OAKLEY

Marshall's Shadow Book 3

KATHI S. BARTON

This is a work of fiction. Names, characters, places, and incidents are products of the author's imagination or are used fictitiously and are not to be construed as real. Any resemblance to actual events, locations, organizations, or persons, living or dead, is entirely coincidental.

World Castle Publishing, LLC
Pensacola, Florida
Copyright © Kathi S. Barton 2020
Paperback ISBN: 9781953271136
eBook ISBN: 9781953271143
First Edition World Castle Publishing, LLC, September 7, 2020
http://www.worldcastlepublishing.com

Licensing Notes
Cover: Karen Fuller
Editor: Maxine Bringenberg

Chapter 1

Harris walked the hallway while she waited on someone from the police department to come and give her a hand. The locals had their hands full with this one and were more than happy to let her not only take over but to make sure that things were done correctly. So far, all Harris had been able to figure out was that Allison Gray had hit the cook, Lachlan Russell.

It had taken her only a minute after finding a nurse by the name of Dutch Jasper. He and Harris had known each other for a while. A couple of times when she'd been in this very hospital taking care of someone, she'd been able to depend on him to make sure she'd gotten out of the hospital without being seen. Harris didn't know why she trusted the man, but she did. With her life, as it turned out.

"I have copies of all the recordings of the conversation with her boss, a jerk by the name of Lance Gray. He's currently sitting his pretty butt in jail, right alongside his daughter, Allie." Harris asked him for a recap of what had gone down. "Her boss was pissy that Lach had his daughter arrested. He told her—point blank, mind you—that he wasn't paying any of her bills. I have the name of the cop that arrested him. Officer Hamilton heard what he said as well."

"Is there anything else?" Dutch told her about the baby Lach was carrying and that it was her sister's child. "That was very generous of her. Or was it?"

"Not from what I've heard. They bullied Lach into it. You have to meet them only once to know they're not the kind of people who tolerate those they think are lower than them. To me, that isn't a far drop, but then I don't give two hoots about them." Harris laughed. "Lach told me right before they took her into surgery that her sister had told her she wasn't able to carry a baby to term. That's not right. I went to talk to someone about it, on the sly, and they're saying that Rita—that's her sister—didn't want to have to carry a child, but she really wanted one. They're paying half of Lach's medical for her carrying the baby. Half? Like she wanted to carry it. I'm telling you now, Harris, if you were still working, I'd hire you."

She thought about that for the rest of the morning. Dutch was one of the nicest people she had ever encountered on her jobs. For him to want to make these people gone was very telling. Pacing the long hallway on the surgery floor, Harris thought about everything she'd found out about Lach. All of it good news until she found out about the rest of her family.

Her parents were divorced. Frank Russell had taken off about the time Lach had turned four. He'd had enough, apparently, and didn't care to be around people he just couldn't make himself love. Harris didn't know the family as yet, but even hearing about them made her think she didn't blame him. Frank had also tried to get custody of Lach, but Rebecca, his ex-wife, had hired a shark of an attorney and had won the case. Harris wondered if she'd thought she could make Lach into someone like her and Rita. Apparently, it hadn't stuck, because Lach was her own woman and didn't hang around her sister and mother unless necessary.

"Mrs. Marshall? There's a phone call for you. He said it was urgent." She nodded and followed the nurse to the front desk. "I think it's Dutch. He didn't tell me his name, but I think it's him."

"Hello?" It was Dutch, and she had to tell him to calm down three times before she was able to get a word out. "Just take a deep breath and let it out slowly. In and out, Dutch, so I can figure out what the fuck is wrong."

"Did you see today's paper?" She reached for it as it laid on the nurse's station counter. "Frontpage too. I have to tell you, Harris, I never in all my wildest dreams would have thought someone could do this to one of the sweetest people I know. I love you too, girl, but you're not sweet. You're hard."

"Thank you." She asked him to hold on while she opened the paper. "Mother fuck. How the hell did they get this out so quickly? Not to mention, how did the person putting this in the paper get this printed without all the facts? Or any, from what I'm seeing."

Harris told Dutch she'd talk to him later as she stood there reading the article. It was about Lach and her having to be in the hospital. It said she'd tried to kill Allie Gray by throwing a hot dinner at her, and when she'd retaliated, Lach had faked an injury in order to get out of going to jail.

It went on to say she'd been feeding the entire staff dinners every night instead of the patrons of the restaurant. There were accusations about her stealing money from the cash drawer, taking money from the waitstaff in the form of tips, as well as taking home some of the products that the restaurant had ordered.

Taking out her cell phone, Harris called her office. She had three people working on this for her. A lot of shit was going on, and since the locals had turned it over to her, she was free to do whatever was needed. Turned out, when she called her office, she found there were more than the three she had assigned to this, as the things they were finding out were too much for the first men to work on.

"I have a man going to the newspaper office as we speak. He's taking one of the local jurisdictions with him. The article was out before we knew about it. Sorry about that, sir." She told him it wasn't his fault, as she'd been blindsided by it as well. "You should also be aware that we've found Frank Russell. He's remarried. A background on him didn't show anything other than one parking ticket. How would you like us to work this?"

"Call him. Tell him his daughter has been hurt. Don't give him any details until he asks for them. I'm not keeping them from him, but if he's broken all contact with them, he might not care." Agent Gunn told her he could do that. She could hear the pen scratching across the paper. "I want you to do a complete background on Lachlan Russell. I have some personal information, but not much more. I want to know the last time she had a shit; that's how thorough I want it. Also, on her mother, Rebecca Russell, and her sister and brother-in-law, Rita and Roger Underwood. Make sure you find out what you can about her ability to have children."

"Got it." He paused a moment. "I know Rita Underwood." She asked him how. "We were upperclassmen together. I didn't realize that when I started helping you with this. To say she's a bitch doesn't even come close to painting a picture of this woman. I think she'd murder her own family if she would be able to make some cash off it."

"Do you know Dutch Jasper?" He said he did, but only by name. He was younger than him. "He's a good friend and ally of Lach. Also, the one that called me. See what you can find out about him, too, while we're looking. Also, what his debt to income ratio is."

She didn't have to explain herself to this man, but she told him he'd helped Lach out and had helped Harris a few times as well. Harris just wanted to know if he was being paid off to make the family look bad. But really, she was going to help the nurse out if he needed it. Harris owed the man a great deal.

"Sir, did you know what Lachlan means? It means warlike. The Vikings called their land of lakes Lachlan too." Harris told him she'd not known, but was glad for the information. "I hope this girl is warlike. Having a sister like Rita, she'd need it."

The more she found out about this family, the more she wanted to bundle up Lach and take her home with her. She wasn't prone to taking adults home with her, but in this, she thought her and the other woman could be tight as in friends. Harris didn't know why, but she thought this Lach might be more badass than she was. Not by much, though.

When Lach came out of surgery, Harris was able to go and see her. The doctor told her what had happened in the operating room, and the concerns he had about what he'd had to do to remove the large shard of glass from her head.

"It was deep and pierced her skull. I could see the damage to her brain—it has a deep cut in it. The brain surgeon with me said she thought that having it cut in her frontal lobe might cause her some memory issues, as well as a change to her personality." Harris asked the doctor how they'd figure it out. "We'll have to wait until she's awake. Which isn't going to be for a few more hours. I'd like her to remain still for at least that long."

Pulling out her cell phone, Harris looked up what she could about frontal lobe injuries. There was a lot, she could see, that was all speculation about the brain. It would be difficult, she supposed, to have someone test your working brain before you were finished with it. In her field, Harris was sure there were a lot of people out there that didn't have a brain. Or, in fact, they didn't use it all that much. She was smiling when she made her way to recovery to sit with Lach for some quiet time.

Opening her laptop, she pulled up the information she had been sent from her office. It was about the recording that had been generated from here, as well as from the restaurant. Allie was going to be in deep shit when this thing went to trial. Having admitted that she wanted to kill the other woman was right there for anyone to hear.

Harris looked at the other recording and cringed when she saw the mother and sister. Typical rich women that wouldn't do a thing for anyone in need, she thought. The fact that the mom was more concerned about her shower and going home told her a great deal. Closing those down, she pulled up the first report.

Allison Gray had been in trouble like this before. As she read over the three counts of abuse and battery from the police, Harris had to wonder how she'd even been able to be out and around others. Her violent nature was one that should have been recognized and monitored before now. Then she got to the records that told the outcome of each of the crimes.

Daddy was paying the people off. Charges were brought against his daughter, but after Lance paid the people a great sum of money, Allison was set free. The amounts were staggering too. Two of them were upwards of a million dollars. The last one was nearly two mill. Harris read the reports on what had happened and noticed that with each arrest, Allison was getting more and more violent. Harris did wonder how much he'd pay Lach to shut her up. She also wondered if she'd take it. Hoping she wouldn't, Harris looked at the woman laying in the bed next to her.

She knew from the report that her left arm had been burnt badly. She could see that it had been wrapped up but was seeping. The one at her back had been the worst the doctor had seen on someone. It was about two feet wide and almost that long. The pain while it healed would be horrendous.

Harris couldn't see much of her face. From the top of her head to her nose, just peeking out of the bandage, she could see that there were bloodstains on the gauze. She was being monitored and had several IV's running to keep her quiet, as the doctor had said. When a nurse came in to take Lach's blood pressure, she told Harris what she knew.

"They had to remove nineteen pieces of glass from her head. Some of them were so tiny, I was told that they had to be found with a microscope." She asked about the one that had caused the skull injury. "Doctor Sampson is the best brain surgeon around. She's a ballbuster, but good at her job. She was telling us the piece that had done the most damage was about an inch wide, and sharp like a razor on the end that hit her. She's lucky that none of the flying glass hit her in the eye."

"I'm sure she's just glad to be alive. Did anyone mention the baby?" The nurse told her the OBGyn would be in later to examine her. "But they didn't say anything about it? I mean, to even tell if the meds might hurt it?"

"No." The nurse came closer to her. "She'll be lucky to keep the baby once she's awake. I've seen what this sort of stress can do to a mother. Lach is going to be in a great deal of pain when she wakes up. Being with child, she won't be able to take the good medication that will keep the pain at bay. I feel sorry for her. And for the unborn child. This will be hard for her to handle on top of being hurt like this."

After the nurse left, Harris watched Lach breathing. Her thoughts were centered on a single thing right now, but executing them might cause more trouble than Lach might want. Harris didn't want her to lose the child. Even if it weren't hers, she thought that the pain of that would put her into a deep depression. She'd seen enough of that for several lifetimes and wanted to keep Lach from having that weight on her as well. Harris nodded at her thoughts and put out an all call to her new family.

I need Rodney and the other three unmated Marshalls to come to the hospital for me. I have a woman here that is going to be in a great deal of pain, and I don't want her to suffer. There is also an unborn child that I'm thinking of. She told them what was going on with the baby, as well as her reasons for asking them to come here. Harris also warned them about her mother and sister troubles. *She might well be one of your mates. In fact, I'm hoping she is. You could make her life a great deal better than it is at the present time.* Harris smiled when Grandpa spoke first.

I'm coming too. If she ain't one of these knuckleheads' mate, I might can heal her myself. Poor things. To think that — Hey, is this the girl I was reading about in the paper here? Where she tried to kill off the owner's daughter? Harris told him she was having that retracted. *I don't blame you. It sure didn't paint her in a good light for all the things they were saying about her. I'll be riding up with the others — no point in me sitting here waiting on someone to tell me what's going on with her.*

I'm going to drive up. Anyone want to ride with me? The other three and Grandpa said they would ride up with Oakley. *Just so you know, I'm not going to be happy if she is my mate. It's not fair that you get to meet her before I do. What things could you be telling her, I wonder?*

She's in a coma right now, medical. They want her to remain stable for as long as she can. Oakley said he was kidding. *I know that. I just wanted to give you all a rundown on what we might be dealing with. I'll keep you updated as I find out more about her. Oh, if you hear about someone being murdered, don't worry about it. I might have saved you the trouble of meeting your in-laws.*

They were still laughing when she closed the connection. Harris was glad now that she'd contacted them. If nothing else, they'd keep her entertained. Pulling out her computer again, she read the other reports that had come in with the first one. This was a family that needed to be beaten, Harris thought.

~*~

Frank made his way up to the fourth floor of the imposing hospital. It wasn't as if he'd not been in a hospital before, but this one was much larger than he'd thought, even with different buildings attached to one another with complicated walkways and bridges. He finally made it to the correct floor twenty minutes after arriving. Frank made his way to the nurse's station to ask where he needed to go.

"Mr. Russell, my name is Harris Marshall with the FBI." He took the younger woman's hand while his mind pinged all over the place about what his ex-wife had done now. "They're setting your daughter up in a room right now. My family is in there helping. I'll take you to see your daughter in a moment. If you don't mind, I have a few questions for you."

"Of course. But if you don't mind me asking, what has

Rebecca done now? Or is it Rita again?" Agent Marshall told him they were still looking into that. "They're not the brightest tools in the shed if you want my opinion. Not only that, but they think they're better than anyone. Not most, but anyone they come in contact with. How's my daughter doing?"

"Lach is doing as well as can be expected. She was burnt badly. But that's nothing to what was done to her brain when a plate was thrown at her. They're waiting to make any kind of prognosis until she's in less pain. The medication she's on is making sure she's not hurting, but is also not harming the baby."

"Baby? Lach is pregnant? No one told me— Well, I guess I never expected anyone to call me on that, but it would have been nice." Agent Marshall told him what she knew. "That's not true. When I was still living with them, Rita had gotten pregnant three times by the time she was seventeen. She carried one to term without any issues. That one was put up for adoption. I suppose there could have been problems starting after I left there, but I'm not aware of any issues she had."

"I've done some research on the family, and you're right. There are no issues for Rita not to have been able to carry a child. Someone on my team thinks it's because she doesn't want to be pregnant." Frank told the agent he didn't believe that either. That Rita thrived on having all the attention focused on her. "Could it be that she is trying to hurt her sister in some way?"

"I wouldn't know. I do know Lach wasn't anything like her sister or mother. I tried to have her come to live with me after the divorce, but Rebecca wouldn't have it. I think, and this is just me, she thought she could turn her into a person like her and my other daughter. I never thought it would stick. Even as a child, Lach was more boy-like than any boy I knew at her age. And stubborn." Frank thought about that. "I guess things could have changed, as I said, but I don't think it would have been easy on my wife or daughter. Lach is very stubborn."

He was talking with Harris, as he'd been asked to call her when a man came out of the room he thought his daughter was in. After kissing Harris on the mouth, the big man introduced himself to him as her husband. Good lord, he'd never seen a pair so perfectly matched before. Tall and muscled. It made him wish he'd used the gym membership he had more.

Shep seemed like a good man. He had a dry wit and was so in love with his wife Frank could almost taste it. Other men came out of the room one at a time, all of them introducing themselves to him as a brother to the one before. Then an older man, who said he was their grandda, Sheppard, introduced himself to him. This man he thought he could enjoy talking to.

"My family here is trying to make sure nothing more happens to your little girl. Harris here, she's told us what is going on, and who we should be looking out for. I don't think there is much going on right now, but we got your back." Frank thanked Sheppard. "You're welcome. I do want to ask you something before much longer here. Do you believe in shifters? I mean, people having another self?"

"My wife was a wolf." Sheppard told him they were jaguars. "Jaguars are beautiful cats. I'm happy to meet all of you. You must have an enormous food bill to feed all these boys, as you call them. I'd hate to have to feed them all at one time."

"They're good boys, Mr. Russell. The reason I said anything at all right now is that your little girl is the mate to one of my grandsons." Frank wasn't sure how to take that, so he said nothing. "My boys here, any one of them would save her from hurting so badly, as she's gonna. But Harris here, she wanted them to come along and see if any of them were her mate before we doctored her up with a little of our blood."

"You're not going to help her now?" Sheppard told him they couldn't, but Oakley could. "I don't understand. How is he going to help her? And what does her being this man's mate have to do with it?"

"Cats are a jealous lot. Wolves too. Had any one of them tried to save her, Oakley would have killed them. He'd not want to, but it's in his DNA to protect what he would consider his own." Sheppard asked him if he was understanding. Frank told him to go on. "Oakley, he's staying with her right now on account of you being here. He wants your permission, you see, to take care that she's not hurt anymore."

The monitors went off down the hall. They were loud and scary. It occurred to him that they were saying that the room his daughter was in was the one the staff was rushing to. Standing up, he was asked to wait as all the staff gathered in the room. A tall, good looking man came out just as the door was closing.

No one said anything for a long time. Then the man he assumed was Oakley came toward him with his hand out. After introductions were made, Frank found himself sizing the younger man up. Whatever had happened in Lach's room, it had affected the young man quite badly.

"She was awake for about a minute before she said anything. As you can imagine, I was shocked to see her awake when they told us it would be a few more days before they started weaning her off the meds." Sheppard asked him why the staff was in the room. "She told me to call them. That she thought she was losing the baby."

Frank sat down. He'd not seen his daughter in twenty years and knew he'd missed a great deal. But the child he remembered was now losing her child. It hurt him deeply that she was going through this. Especially, he thought, with so much going on right now in her life.

"How about you and me, we go and get us some dinner, Frank?" He started to tell Sheppard no, that he wanted to stay close to see his daughter when Sheppard continued. "You don't want to go and see her like you're looking right now. You're hurting, I can see that. I am too, and I've not met her yet. But a good cup of tea or coffee with a piece of pie might do wonders for you. It'll also give you time to figure out what to say to her when it's time to talk."

"I suppose you might be right. I was wondering why the FBI was in on this. Seems like it would be a local thing." As Sheppard explained it to him, Frank found himself not only going with Sheppard to the cafeteria but also ordering himself two pieces of pie and a cup of coffee. When he sat down with the other man, Harris and her husband joined them. He had a feeling he was going to learn a great deal about his other family.

"All right, Frank. How do you want this? Rip the sucker right off, or do you want it in bits and pieces? I'm more of a rip it off sort of teller, but I'll do what you need." He said he wasn't sure what he wanted, as he'd not been around for twenty years. "I'm here because a friend of mine called me in. Dutch Jasper, he's not only a friend of mine but also your daughter. Do you remember him?"

"Yes. I mean, I remember the name and a little about him. Dutch would come over when they were little and hang out with the family when his mom had to work late. My then wife didn't like him. I haven't any idea why, but it didn't stop him and Lach from being friends. He called you because she'd been hurt?" Harris told him that was part of it. "Why then? I mean, if you can tell me."

"Have you seen the papers?" He said not since he

left home last night. The paper was handed to him. After reading it, he looked at Harris. "None of that is true. Well, some of it is. Lach was burnt, but not how they describe it. We're having a retraction put out tomorrow. Fact-checking is a biggy for me. Also, we've arrested Allison and her father, as well as a med student, for taking pictures and sending them to the father and daughter duo."

Harris told him of the other attempts of murder by Allison, as well as her father buying the victims off. His head was spinning when he thought of all the things going on surrounding this other family. Asking for a moment, Harris didn't say anything more other than she was sorry.

"Don't be. I'm just thinking how very little I knew before coming here. So this, all this with my daughter being hurt, was over a fake order so Allison could have a steak dinner? What is this world coming to?" Harris said she asked the same question every day. "I bet you do. You more than likely see very little good come out of your job."

"I see the good when I have someone in jail for something. But this, it should never have been allowed to happen. Someone's head is going to roll for this. Allison is a danger to people and has been for some time. I'm going to make sure justice is served for Lach." Frank asked about the baby. "When I came down here, the staff was still in the room. Oakley went back in too. He'll let me know when he knows anything."

They told him what they knew, which wasn't a small amount. Harris and her family not only knew what Rita had done to her sister to make her carry her unborn child but also how Rita was making sure she only paid half of what it was costing Lach to do this for her.

"The contract I saw wasn't signed by Lach. There is a signature in the line where she was supposed to sign, but your ex-wife signed it. Then she wrote that Lach wasn't of sound mind. I find that hard to believe, but that's what happened. Rita and her husband have been spending money like they're drinking it, and they're not planning to pay Lach for any of this. You'll have to trust me on that one, Frank. I can't tell you who told me that, but it's straight from Rita's mind." Frank could believe that. Rebecca and Rita both hated when they were told no on something. "I can believe that too. The two of them are like two she devils fighting over a tiny pea. I don't think either of them are aware of what sort of shit is going to rain down on them now that I've had a look into their lives."

"Explain to me how it is you're involved. You might say you came here for a friend to make sure my daughter wasn't screwed, but I think it's more than that. Something you're not telling me." Harris nodded. "Is it bad? Is it something I'm going to regret knowing?"

"I doubt that last part. However, I am here for a friend. Once I got here, things changed a great deal, but that is why I came. So I could see that someone wasn't getting shafted." He said he still thought there was more. "There is. The fact that this girl tried to kill Lach pisses me off. Then to find out she could have killed the mate to one of my brothers makes me want to see bloodshed."

"I have a feeling you're good at making bloodshed anyway." They all laughed, and Harris patted him on the back. "I want you to know this, Harris—I'm not going to piss you off in any way. I don't want to be on the receiving end of your wrath."

"Smart man."

She pulled out a gun and laid it on the table. He didn't think she was showing off but had put it there because, as she said, it was digging into her hip. For whatever reason, Frank didn't think Harris had to show off. She was that good at what she did.

Chapter 2

Oakley read over the paperwork he'd been given by the doctor. Doctor Shipley was one of the two men that had operated on Lach. The other doctor, Doctor Wagner, was the one who was caring for the child Lach still carried.

"Do I know you?" He looked at the bed and smiled at the woman there. They had removed the bandages from her head, and now only her forehead and left eye were covered up. "I don't think I know who the hell you are, do I?"

"You don't. I'm Oakley Marshall." She asked him if that was supposed to impress her. "Not that I know of. I'm here with my sister-in-law, Harris Marshall, to make sure you don't get into any more trouble than you are right now. Also, to make sure things don't go as planned by your sister and mother."

"They're pieces of work. I really don't want to ask,

but what do you know about the baby? You were in here before, so I'm assuming you might know about the baby." He told her what the doctor had told him. "I don't think I'm going to be getting up and doing any kind of jig for a while yet. But why the hell did he tell you? I'm assuming we're not related in any way. Like marriage or worse?"

"I started to ask you why you thought marriage would be bad, but I've been reading about the divorce proceedings of your parents. Your mother isn't a nice person at all, is she?" Lach told him he was right on that score. "The baby is fine. The bleeding, he said, is from all the stress. That if you don't get stressed out anymore, you should be fine. I'm to tell you that when you want something, there is pain medication for you."

"You're not human." He said he wasn't, and told her what he was. "I have two buddies that aren't human. Berkeley is the dishwasher at the restaurant where I worked. He's a vampire. Old one, too, that doesn't need the job but has a place to hang out when he gets up. Also, CarolAnn. She's a wolf. Her mate died some time ago, and they'd not had any children. She's lonely. I think she's bossy too, but I won't say that to her face. Am I going to be all right?" He told her they both were. "Rita, my sister, she'd have a cow if she thought I might lose this baby. I haven't any idea why, but I really don't know that she wants it. I don't think motherhood is going to be anything like she thinks it's going to be. But that's just me."

"She lied to you." Lach didn't say anything, but he had a feeling she knew that. "Also, you should know that Harris is working on figuring out a few things on the contract. She's really glad you didn't sign anything."

"That didn't matter, now did it?" He asked her what she meant. "I'm still knocked up with this baby. Not that I'd want to hurt it, but it wasn't my first choice to have my first child this way. My husband being the father of the child, would have been my first wish. And not having myself taken for a ride concerning how I got talked into this. The contract was made after I found out I was going to have the baby."

"I didn't think a contract worked that way." She laughed a little but moaned in pain. "There are a couple of more things I need to talk to you about. Some of it isn't all that bad — at least I don't think it is — and then there are some things you should know too."

"My head really hurts. Is that normal?" Oakley told her about the brain wound as well as the stitches to put her forehead back together. "I feel like they might well have left the drill in there when they were finished up. Can you call out or something to see what they can give me? I'm getting sick, it hurts so much."

Oakley picked up the nurse call button and called for the nurse. She must have been on her way in because she was there within moments. As Lach was given something for pain in her IV, he waited for the nurse to leave to ask

Lach if she wanted any more information. He never got a chance to ask her because as soon as the drug hit her system, she was out.

Making notes for himself had always been something Oakley did. Things that he needed to do for the day, the things he might have to pick up around town, and also a grocery list. He even made notes when he had to talk to someone about something. It made him feel secure that he was using his time, and that of the person he had to talk to, in the best possible way. At the top of his list for Lach was telling her that they were mates.

When the nurse came back in to check on Lach, he stood up to stretch. Oakley was surprised to realize it was nearly dinner time. Asking the nurse how much longer she thought Lach would be sleeping, he figured he had more than enough time to run down to get himself smoothing to eat. Suddenly he was starving.

The cafeteria was nice. There were a lot of people in it, so he figured the food would be good. Once he decided on a couple of sandwiches, as well as some chips and bottled water, he was on his way back to her room.

Lach was awake. A nurse, not the one from earlier, was reading his note to Lach.

Sitting down, he didn't interrupt the two of them. He figured it was just a list — how much trouble could he be in? As soon as the nurse left them, Lach called him a mother fucker. Things, he figured, were about to get bad.

"Why would you tell me in a note that we're mates?

If that isn't the most childish thing I've ever heard of." He said it was his list. That he always made lists. "How the hell does that make it any better? You made me a list to read over?"

"No. I made me a list of things I wanted to tell you. It wasn't for you, but so I'd not be remiss in letting you know things you might want to know." She huffed at him. "I haven't any idea what that might mean, but if you had turned the list over, you would have noticed I also had a grocery list, as well as one of the things for me to do when I get home. No hurry on those things, in the event you want me to stick around with you." He could tell she was still upset, but he didn't comment on it.

"I don't know what's going on. My head feels explosive. My arm hurts, and I feel like my back is going to burn through my spine and come out on top of me." She looked at him, tears streaming down her cheek from her one good eye. "They told me I could have more medication, but you have no idea how terrified I am of hurting this baby."

"Babies." She asked him what he meant. "Twins. I can tell you also that one of them is a girl, the other, of course, is a boy. They're healthy too, and while they do get some of the drugs you're taking, it's not harmed them so far."

"Twins. You're sure? What am I saying? Of course, you're sure." She put her hands on her small belly. "The doctor didn't tell me that. He said the baby was small. I guess I know why now. Why wasn't that on your list?"

"I didn't know if you knew or not. My lists are stuff I need to do or tell someone." He smiled at her. "If you're really nice to me, I can give you some ice water. They said you could have some."

"Not yet." She started to cry again. "I feel so emotional all the time. You think it's from having twins?"

"I don't know the answer to that one. I could ask my brother Rodney for you. He's a doctor." Lach said that would be nice. "There are other things I could help you with. It wasn't on the note because I wanted to make sure you were aware of me being your mate. But I can heal you."

"Seriously?" He told her he didn't have much of a sense of humor most of the time. He didn't get sarcasm either. "I bet that goes over well with the people you live with. How would you heal me? Exactly. I don't want you to tell me this in bits and pieces, and I still get surprised at the end."

"As my cat—I did tell you I was a jaguar, right? As my cat, I could lick the wound on your back and arm and take care of those, so they heal up. The one on your forehead, that one I would have to ask about. But—and I'm not pushing this, because again, I don't know how it will affect your condition—I could change you into a cat. That is a little more dangerous. However, with you being ill already, it might be quicker for you. I'd have to ask my grandda. He's been around the longest and would know." Lach didn't say anything for several minutes as he ate one of his sandwiches. When she turned to look at him, he paused in taking a bite to see if he was going to have to answer her quickly or not. "Are you all right?"

"I don't know. Can I tell you something?" He told her she could tell him anything. "All right, but you might not be so thrilled with it once I tell you. What if I told you I can see things? Things I'm betting no one else can see."

He looked around the room but didn't comment. All sorts of things raced through his mind, but none of them were anything he wanted to ask her about. Putting down his meal, he got up and sat on the side of the bed, careful of not turning her in a way that would cause her pain.

"While I haven't any idea what you can see, I want you to know I support you in any way you need. Whatever it is, we'll deal with it. Is it dead people?" He didn't know where that question came from, but when she nodded, he felt his heart race just a little. "Are they in the room with us now? I mean, they don't want to hurt you, do they?"

"Just like that. You believe me?" He asked her if there was a reason he shouldn't. "I don't know. I guess not. But no, they don't seem to want to hurt me. There are two of them in here now. I have a feeling one of them killed the other and then himself."

Taking her hand into his, he felt her squeeze his hand back. Trying to think about what he should do now, he looked in the direction she was looking. He didn't see anyone, but that didn't mean much. They'd not bonded or even touched all that much. Turning back to Lach when she said his name, he could see she was as confused as he was.

"Do you think this has anything to do with the hole in my head?" He didn't know and said that to her. "They're talking to me, Oakley. They're telling me I can talk to them. I'm scared shitless right now. I just want you to talk to me. About anything. Your list. Tell me about your list for the store."

"I need to get some milk. I just eat cereal in the morning, but I'd change that up if someone were there with me. I like to cook." He thought of where she'd been when she'd gotten hurt. "You like to cook? I'm not assuming you do. Just because you work in a restaurant, that doesn't mean you enjoy putting together—"

"You're babbling." He smiled and then leaned down and kissed her on the mouth. "That was tricky of you. I'm calmer now. The man that has been shot said he'd like me to tell the police where his body is. The smell, he said, will not be pleasant much longer. The other man— he said he was his brother—told me I'm not to do that. He'll be in trouble."

"Does he realize he's dead, and there isn't much more trouble he can get in?" Her laughter made him smile. "Ask him why they did this. I mean, was there a problem that led to them being dead?"

Oakley didn't know if it was morbid of him to be

enjoying himself, but he was. Lach spoke to the men and nodded several times before she looked at him. There was something very charming about her smile, which made him want to make her smile all the time.

"His name is Taylor. He doesn't remember his last name. The killer is Carl. Taylor said they're both ill. They've been trying to make it on what is coming in each month, but their medications are more than they can pay. Poor guys. I wish I could have helped them." Oakley said he did as well. "They're at their home. But since neither of them knows their last name, I'm not sure what we should do."

"I'll contact Harris. She's head of the FBI around here. Perhaps she can figure it out." He reached out to her and told her what was going on. Even telling her that Lach was calmer now that he was there, and figuring out that she could see the dead. *So, if you could keep this under wraps for a little while, at least until she gets used to it, I'll be forever grateful.*

I don't even know what to say to this. I'm looking it up now. Do you suppose that since they found her, they're close? I mean, that would— When Harris paused, he waited too. *Ask Lach if one of the men can tell her if their last name is Howard. If so, then I found their address. Christ, Oakley. She might be right on this. They've not been seen in three days, according to the local reports I've tapped into.*

"Taylor said that was his last name. Howard. They're both very happy that they know it now." She looked at him after a few minutes passed. "Ask Harris if she'll be careful of going to the house. Carl was afraid he'd not be able to kill himself, so he rigged the house. Tell her to go into the house from the basement, and he'll tell her — he'll tell me, then I'll tell her how to disarm the bomb he made. I don't think she should do this, Oakley. It's dangerous."

After explaining to Harris what Lach had said, Oakley laughed when she started cursing. It was funny to hear her do it too because Harris was that good at cursing. Some of the words he thought she was making up as she ran out of ones she knew. By the time she was ready to speak again, he'd told Lach what was going on. Lach had a wonderful laugh too.

Okay. I have a team of men with me. Tell Lach I'm going to be careful, but she is as well. I don't know how the hell she's doing this, but she more than likely saved a lot of lives by warning me.

It took Harris ten minutes to get her team ready to go in. Once she was ready, Oakley relayed what was being said to Lach to Harris as to where to find the bomb. Oakley knew the exact moment Harris found it. He could feel her terror. When she spoke to him, it was nothing more than a whisper.

You tell Lach I'm going to give her a big fat kiss when I see her. This bomb would have taken out the whole neighborhood around here, it's that big. He told Lach, who also looked worried. *All right. I'm ready. Just please don't tell Shep about where I am. Not until I'm out of here. If I get out of here.*

It took the longest five minutes of any of their lives for Harris to say the bomb had been disarmed. The bomb squad was called, and they were on their way when he felt Harris's relief. It was so profound he knew his brother had to have felt it as well.

Kissing the back of Lach's hand, he told her the bomb squad was on their way. She, too, was relieved, and laid her head back on the pillow behind her and cried. Relief, she told him — she was so relieved she couldn't contain it.

~*~

Lach had asked that Oakley be with her when she spoke to her mom and sister. She didn't know how they were going to take having twins, but Lach was very excited for them. Twins. One of each. It would be like a dream come true for her.

Not that she'd ever thought of having children. In fact, she'd not once thought of even being pregnant with her own child until she'd met Oakley. Not having any idea what she was going to do about them being mates, she was willing to think about it. He smiled at her when she'd said that. It made her feel like she'd won the biggest lottery in the entire country.

When he'd left her last night, she laid in the bed alone and thought about calling him back. As she tried to reason with herself, telling herself that they had just met, all she could think about was having him near her. As her door slid open, she could hear him speaking to someone on the other side. Then he was in the room with her.

"Don't leave." He said he didn't have to. "I don't know why, but I want you to stay here with me. I'm sorry I'm selfish about you having to sit in that uncomfortable chair all night, but I can't stand the thought of being alone."

"I can find out if I can have another chair, and that way, I can at least prop my feet up." He didn't tell her no, he wasn't staying. Not once did he give her a look like he wasn't going to at least put up a fight. Instead, he went out of the room and came back a few minutes later. Not only did he have another chair, but he had two pillows and a blanket too. "They said I could stay if it kept you happy. I'm glad. I came back to see if I could steal a goodnight kiss and to pick up my list, but this is so much better."

"I want you to heal me." He told her he could do that. "But not until I speak to my sister and mother. I guess Roger, her husband, is coming in as well. I don't particularly care for him. I call him oily, but I'm not married to him. Thankfully."

"I would love to marry you someday soon." She giggled, feeling light and free for the first time in a long time. Lach asked him about that. "You're safe, and you know it. I think it also has a lot to do with us being meant for each other. I know I feel better since I met you. Sort of like I've gotten all my ducks in a row, and I can sleep well."

"That's how I feel too. Like everything is aligned." He set up his bed while asking her about a home. "I only have a little apartment. It's not big—you'd make it seem smaller too, I'm thinking. But whatever you have now is fine with me."

"I want a home. Do you have any sort of rights to visit your babies?" She told him she'd never even thought of asking that. "If you have your contract someplace where I can have someone look it over, I know some pretty savvy attorneys. One of them works for Harris, so you know he's good."

"I'd like that. I've never signed it. I should also tell you I was tricked into carrying her babies. My mom forged my name to the paperwork the doctor needed to impregnate me. They lined it all up, so when I went in for my yearly exam, things were ready for them to do their thing. I did wonder why I had to take such heavy doses of vitamins before I went in. I just assumed with the bloodwork that had also been ordered, they found out that I was deficient in something." Oakley asked her if she wanted to sue them. "I've actually been thinking about it. I mean, to hear Rita talk about this whole thing, it was life or death for her. Then I found out from a friend of mine that there isn't anything wrong with Rita at all."

The door opened, and she stared at the man in the doorway. She didn't know him, so looked at Oakley when he stood up. The man, an older gentleman, was staring at her like she was something he'd never seen before.

"Hello, Lachlan, my darling. You've grown up." She didn't know the man. Nothing about him was familiar. When he smiled at her, however, Lach sat up straighter in the bed and hurt herself. "Don't do that, child. My goodness, just lie still. If you want, I can go and come back some other time. I've been trying to work up the nerve to come see you for a couple of days now, but I didn't know how you'd feel about that. So tonight, I told myself that if you were sleeping, I'd just—"

"Dad." Lach heard his teeth snap close. "I'm sorry I didn't know who you were at first. I'm glad to see you. It's been so long."

He took her hand and hugged it to his face. "I've been hearing all sorts of things about you. The newspaper surely did paint you in a different picture the first time I read about your being hurt." She didn't know what he was talking about but nodded. "Harrison Marshall called me and told me that you had been hurt. Then she went on to tell me it was well past time that I came to see you. She's a very pushy woman."

Oakley laughed and said she was. "Harris is my sister-in-law. She is head of the FBI in this area. Here, take one of my chairs." Her dad sat down but didn't let go of her hand. "If you two don't mind, I'm going to—"

Both she and her dad told him no at the same time. Oakley laughed and sat back down. Lach didn't know what to say to her dad, so she told him how she'd ended up in the hospital. He seemed to know all about that.

"Harris. She's been keeping me updated on things. I wanted to come to see you sooner, honey, but I didn't know what sort of reaction I'd get from you. I know your mother and sister won't be happy about me being around. I didn't care what they thought. It was you that I was concerned about." Lach told him she was glad to see him. "Thank you. You've no idea how much I've thought about you over the years. I wish now I'd fought harder in keeping you with me. You were never going to be anything like the two of them."

The three of them talked until she had to get her blood pressure taken again. The nurse said it was coming down, which made her happy, and that her temperature had gone down a degree. She told her that she'd take what she could get.

Dad stood up when the nurse left. "I should go back to my hotel for a little while. I've not been sleeping well, thinking about how you would react to me being around. I have a feeling I'll sleep like a baby tonight." Dad kissed her on the cheek, then shook hands with Oakley. "Thank you for being here with my little girl. She is one of the best."

"I know that too, sir." After her dad left, she asked Oakley if he could ring for the nurse. She was in a great deal of pain right now. "You'll need to stop putting it off—the meds, I mean. It's easier for you to get smaller doses than one large one if you keep taking them on time."

"The nurse told me the same thing. But I don't want to miss anything." She laid back when the nurse came in and watched Oakley as she was drugged up. "Oh my, that feels so much better."

"Close your eyes, Lach. Let them take you under." She did as he told her. "Before you nod off, where are Carl and Taylor?"

"They disappeared when Harris told us the bomb was disarmed. I think they just wanted someone to take care of them." She yawned again, feeling the pull of her burns on her back. "Tomorrow, I'd like for you to fix me up, Oakley. I don't want to hurt like this anymore. Can you ask your grandda about it?"

"I will, love." She was fighting to stay awake. The pain was still there, but it was muted now like someone had started to make it better and was still working on it. "I'm in love with you, Lach. I wanted you to know that as you slumber. Tomorrow I will make sure you're not in as much pain, and then I'll get to take you home with me. I have a home I'm working on right now. It's not anywhere close to being finished. Would you like to go house hunting with me too? I would rather, to be honest, have a house that the two of us picked out together."

She wanted to answer him but couldn't make her mouth move. There were sounds of moving furniture, and she knew he was getting ready for slumber too.

What a funny word, slumber. Lach decided she'd call it that from now on. Going to slumber sounded so much more relaxing than going to bed. Tomorrow, she thought. Things would be better tomorrow.

Something woke her. The nurse or whoever they were told her they were taking her blood pressure again. She spoke to Oakley quietly, but she didn't understand what they were saying. It took her only seconds to fall back to sleep.

It happened again. This time she was awake enough to know her blood pressure was fine, and her temp had gone down again. They had been worried about her getting an infection. Lach was grateful for that news. She looked at the shadow standing over her as her arm was being unwrapped from the bandage.

"I'm going to fix your arm for you now. You've been moaning in your sleep about how it hurts. All right?" Nodding, she let him take her arm and lay it over her bed. "Don't freak out if you see my cat, honey. He's going to take the pain away for you."

She wanted to see his cat, but he explained to her that someone might see him if she were to turn on the lights. Agreeing with him, she felt the room tighten, like she had been squeezed, then felt his warm tongue on her wound.

Looking at the cat beside her bed, she was surprised at how big he was. His eyes glowed brightly in the room, and she reached out with her other hand and scratched him behind his ears. The purring made her laugh a little.

"I didn't know that big cats purred. You sound like a well-oiled machine." He told her he thought all cats, no matter the size, purred. Then Oakley explained to her that he was going to wrap her arm back up until after her family left. "Good. I don't know what they'll say to me if I'm suddenly well. They'll say I've been faking it, I think."

Her mind was a little fuzzy when she felt the bandage being wrapped around her arm. Moving her fingers, it didn't hurt all that much. Before Oakley, she couldn't even point with that hand. Closing her eyes again, she fell asleep knowing in the morning she'd have Oakley close by if she needed him.

Chapter 3

Oakley was looking out the window when the door behind him opened. He didn't know who the man was, so he asked him if he could help him. The look he gave him made even Oakley's cat snarl. He didn't know why, but he immediately knew it had to be Lach's brother-in-law.

"Who the fuck are you?" Oakley let just enough of his cat go to show the man he wasn't going to tolerate being spoken to like that. "Where is my sister?"

"Since I haven't any idea who you are, I couldn't tell you where she might be. Even if you had one." Roger rolled his eyes and asked where Lach was. "They took her down to X-ray about an hour ago. They're making sure the nick to her skull hasn't caused her any swelling to her brain."

"And you are?" Oakley was tempted to tell him it was none of his business but told him his name. That was all too. He didn't feel he should have to explain himself to anyone. "Why are you in her room? And don't fob me off, either. I have a connection to her, and I won't have you hanging around making trouble for us."

"I don't know if you're aware of this or not, but Lach is a grown woman. She can and does make decisions on her own. Between the two of us, I'm positive that if it came down to one of us being kicked out, it wouldn't be me." The man snorted at him, and Oakley laughed. "You're not too terribly grown up yourself, are you?"

When the door opened again, he knew this was her mother and sister. He didn't like them any better than he did Roger. Rita ignored him in favor of bitching about the size of the room. Her mother talked about all the flowers in the room and checked to see if they were for Lach or not.

"I could have sworn she didn't have anyone who would care enough to send her flowers. I'm sure they've put them in here to make her room better. It certainly could use some improvement." Rebecca looked at him. "Why don't you go out and find us some more seating? Once you have us enough chairs to go around, then you can leave. I don't want you around here while my daughter is here. Rita doesn't need you upsetting her."

"No." Oakley took one of the two chairs in the room and looked at the others. "I don't know that you can get any more chairs in this room once Lach is back with her bed. But if you want to, you can ask one of the nurses."

"He told me he's going to be staying no matter what I tell him to do. Rebecca, if she's going to be hanging out with riffraff, then I'm going to have to have a conversation with her about our child." Rebecca told Roger he might have to. The three of them ignored him over talking amongst themselves. "Where the hell is she? Doesn't she know we hate to be kept waiting? I bet she scheduled this so we'd have to wait in here like we have nothing else to do today."

I have a question for you. He told Harris what he was currently doing and who was with him. *Good for you. Roger is a prick. I've been talking to some of the people that work with him, and he's not a very good boss. If he worked for me, I'd have his ass fired. You know what, I think I'm going to own his ass here in a few minutes. My question for you. There is a house not far from our home that has just become vacant. Before you ask, no, I didn't have anything to do with it. But I will tell you if you get it, I'm going to be super jealous. It's beautiful.*

They talked about the price and the size of the place. It also had several outbuildings with it, plus a large garden that was bigger than the one they had on their property. What Harris was jealous about was that there was not only a stocked pond on the back of the property, but there were two houses for staff on the property as well.

Will I need staff? She told him he would. With a house that had seven bedrooms, it would be difficult to keep up. *And how do you think I'm going to fill those rooms? In the event you might have missed it, my mate is still in the hospital.*

I know that, dork. But with your grandda making plans to stay over at each of our homes, it would be nice for him to have a bit of space for himself. Or, and this is what Shep said, you could easily let him live in one of the smaller homes, so he has a place to call his own. He liked that idea and told her that. *I'm going to send you some pictures of the house and property. Show them to Lach when her family is gone. Or after you kill them. Whichever you do, you know I have a lot of experience in making it look like an accident.*

This time when the door opened, he knew it was going to be Lach. When she reached for his hand, he took hers into his. She was pale and in a great deal of pain. He knew if her family wasn't there, he'd make sure her back was healed too.

"I need something for pain." Her sister and mother said no at the same time. "Kiss my ass. I'm hurting, and I'm taking care that I don't take too much. Fuck, I hurt."

"Every time I'm around you, I realize what a lowlife you are, Lach. For heaven's sake, don't act like this around me." Her mother went to the other side of the bed and reached for her other hand. Lach jerked away from her. "You ungrateful child. I was just going to offer you some comfort."

"I wondered for a very long time if you knew what that meant. But I don't want you to hold my sore arm, Mother. In case you're forgotten, I've been burned badly." She looked at Oakley. "Please."

He picked up the call button, but before he could ring for the nurse, she came in. Martha had been Lach's nurse yesterday, and Oakley thought she was about the most no-nonsense woman he'd ever met.

"I got you some good juice right here, Lach, honey. You just lay there and let me take the edge off for you." Lach started crying and told her she was sorry. "You don't have to tell me you're sorry, child. I know you had to be beat up pretty badly when they took you away. You just let this fill in the spaces of pain, then you'll be right as rain in no time."

"I don't want her to have anything." Martha huffed at Rita when she spoke. "Did you hear me? She's going to have my baby, and I don't want her to make him stupid by having too much dope in his system."

"Do you, by chance, have a medical degree? Do you happen to know more than I do about such things? You don't. Now, if you don't have anything nice to say here, then you just sit your skinny little butt down and leave me to my work. This child has a hole in her noggin, and I'm betting you'd be begging for something for pain too if it were you. Now, leave me alone." Martha looked at him and winked. "Oakley, I heard your grandda is coming in later. You tell him to come by and see me. I have him some late tomatoes if he wants them."

"I'll do that. He's bringing dinner us. The doctor told us this morning that she can have something on the light side, so he's getting her some soup and bread." Martha, like him, ignored the others in the room. "I think he's bringing you in something as well."

"Your family, they're the best, Oakley. Don't know what your little town down there would do if it wasn't for your generosity." Rita cleared her throat and then asked who he was. "He's the best thing that ever happened to your little sister, if I don't miss my bet."

"He is." He leaned down and kissed Lach on her mouth when she spoke to him. "I'm all right now if you want to sit down. You're wonderful for being here with me."

Roger nearly knocked his wife over racing to get to the other chair. Oakley didn't try to hide his laughter at the man. The idiot was going to have to get up soon anyway. As he said, his grandda was bringing in dinner.

When Martha left them, telling them they weren't to sit on the bed, she winked at him again. He was going to have to do something special for the woman. Oakley thought of all the things she'd made sure he had while staying here, including enough towels for him to shower in Lach's room. As well as a meal for him when the others on the floor were having theirs.

"I'm glad you're here. Well, not really, but now that you are, we can get some things taken care of. First and foremost, I want you to know I'm having my attorney look over the contract you signed for me." Rita asked her why she'd do something like that. "Because of how I ended up carrying your children."

"You won't have to do this again for us, Lach. I wish I hadn't asked you to do it in the first place now. The way you whine and moan about every little thing." Lach pointed out that she'd not been asked at all. "Not that it matters now, but I should have thought things through about what sort of person you are. No. We've only ever wanted one child, and this is all for us."

"I'm glad you brought that up, Rita. You lied to me about not being able to carry a child to term. From talking to Dad, I know you'd not had any trouble at all getting pregnant and carrying the first time you were—"

"You're not to talk to that man." Oakley held tightly onto Lach's hand when her mother got up and stood over her. "He's nothing. Less than nothing, and I won't have you talking to him at all. I forbid it."

"Not that I care what you forbid me to do, but I'll see and talk to whomever I want to. He's my father." When Rita drew back like she was going to hit Lach, Oakley growled. No one in the room moved. "It's all right, Oakley. If she'd hit me, I would have gladly had you toss them out of the room. Sit down, Mother, and shut the fuck up."

"This right here is what I mean about you being unfit to carry my child." Lach said children. "I have already explained to you, Lach, that I'll never allow you to carry another child for me."

"I'm carrying twins, Rita. A boy and a girl." Rita told

her to grow up. "I have no idea why that would be said to me, but that's the truth. There is no direct science on how many eggs get fertilized when you do in vitro. I've been asking the staff here a lot of questions. But I'm having twins for you."

"Then you're going to have to get rid of one of them. I don't want two. You have them abort the girl. I want a son." No one spoke. He even thought Lach's mother was shocked by what Rita said. "You heard me. I only want one of them. I don't care how you do it, but I will not allow you to have two children. No. Do something about it now."

"Do something about it? Are you insane? I can't abort a child because you want only one. What the fuck is wrong with you?" Lach looked at him. "I thought she'd be happy, not a monster like she is. Christ."

"I'm not a monster. I told you when you found out you were pregnant that you were to have me a son, and that was all. I don't want to raise a daughter. I need you to take care that when you have this done, you only take the girl out. Or so help me, Lach, I won't pay you a dime for anything." Oakley could feel the pain coursing through Lach. "I'm going home. You had better have this taken care of before I return. Do you hear me?"

"I'm not going to do anything. I'm going to have two children that you had some quack plant in me, and that's all there is to it. Do you hear me?" Rita moved to the door and called for Roger to come with her. "You're not going to make me do a damned thing, Rita. I'm pregnant with twins. Deal with it."

"I don't want the girl. Whatever you do, you make sure you deliver a son. I'll sue you if you dare bring that girl into this world."

Oakley finally had enough. "Shut the fuck up, you fucking bitch." Rita said she was leaving. "Good. But know this. The moment you walk out that door without settling this with your sister, you'll have to go through me to see the children. They're both coming into this world, and you have two choices. Take them both or neither of them. And you had better never do anything to harm the little girl, either. If you do, I'll come at you so hard you'll wish you had kept your fucking mouth shut."

"Who the hell do you think you are, telling me what I can and can't do? I'll have you know that this is my decision, not yours. Lach, I will speak to you later about this. However, if this is your decision too, then I won't pay for anything for you." Lach said she'd not paid anything as yet, so that wasn't going to be a hardship for her. "Always the smart ass, aren't you? Well, I have news for you, little sister. Let's see how quickly this man here runs out on you. I hope he does. It's exactly what you deserve."

Rita just stood there, her anger evident on her face and in the way she stood stiff and unyielding. When she spoke, her lips moved, but her teeth remained clenched. In that moment, Oakley decided he was going to have

Harris look deeper into the life of this woman. Anger like that didn't just show itself on a whim.

"You are no longer a child of mine. I will never come to speak to you, nor will I have one thing to do with you if you don't do what Rita said." Lach didn't bother saying anything but did lift her chin up to show she wasn't budging. "Fine. Suit yourself. But don't come running to me when things sour for you. I'm washing my hands of you."

After her mother and family left, Lach was inconsolable. She cried so hard that Martha came in to see what had happened to them. After a quick explanation to her about what had happened, she went out of the room only to return with two boxes of tissues and some more medication for her. Lach was still crying softly when the medication took her under again.

~*~

Harris was spitting mad. Not nearly so much as Grandda was, but Harris thought she was about as close to pissed off as he was. It was all she could do not to find her guns and hunt the bitches down. The nerve of some people. Asking again if Oakley needed anything, Harris went into the hall and made some calls. She had made all her calls except to her office, which she did now.

"I've been looking into the names you've given me. Roger Underwood died fifty-one years ago. If there is another one around, I certainly can't find him." She asked him if he found anything with that name for now.

"Yes, sir. I have a driver's license for the name—and address. However, none of that is any more recent than the last ten years—about the time he married Ms. Russell. I am looking into some other information I got from a neighbor. She said she thought someone had come by once looking for a different name than Underwood. Mrs. Rake said she'd call me back when she found the name. She apparently wrote it down."

"I wonder why she did that." Gilbert told her what he'd been told. "So, this elderly lady thinks something is fishy about the couple living next door to her and starts keeping notes. Perhaps we should hire her for some undercover shit."

"I thought of that as well." Gilbert was one of her best men, and he was a good deal more fun to work with than most of the other agents she had. "She's supposed to be letting us use her notes once she lets us know the name. I've sent a courier to her home to get them and also sent a hundred dollars out of petty cash for her help. I hope that was all right."

"Excellent idea. No, that's a great idea. Thank you for doing that. When you get the notes, let me know. I'll come by the office tomorrow and—"

"I'm having them brought straight to you, sir. I know you've been there at the hospital with your friend, and I thought that would save you time." She was going to promote this kid soon if he kept this up. "Also, I have a lead on the sister. She's not nice to her help, so they're ready and willing to share all kinds of juicy stuff with me."

"You are going to have my job soon if you keep this up." He assured her he just wanted to keep right on being able to do research. "I can tell. I'm guessing you didn't get to do this sort of thing much under Jamison, did you?"

"Not a great deal, no. He had everyone doing the same research. Once we all had the same information, he would have us compare notes on it. It wasn't a very good use of our time, I always thought. I liked working for him, don't get me wrong, but he had his own ways of doing things."

After making sure Gilbert had everything he needed, Harris went back into the room with the rest of the family. Lach was still resting, and Oakley had filled them in on what had happened. She had an idea what they could do but wanted to test the waters a little more before she brought it up.

"I'd like to have them right here is what I'd want. Them durn people should have been a good deal nicer to my little girl." Oakley told Grandda he wished he'd had more room and a place to hide the bodies. "You got that right. Poor little thing. I wish I could have been here for her."

"She cried herself to sleep, Grandda. I don't think either me or my cat was very happy with that. Even with the drugs in her system, she still cried off and on. I'm in love with her, and I want to do nothing more than to hurt those that made her cry." Grandda told him he felt the same way. "Have you found anything, Harris?"

"I've been having my office look into things. Before I forget, I've spoken to Ricky about the contract. There are so many loopholes in it he was surprised anyone would want to sign it." Grandda asked her what she meant. "The contract is mostly for the benefit of Rita and Roger. If she does anything wrong, such as gets the flu, gets a tattoo, they can demand that she terminate the pregnancy. And here's the kicker—they can demand that at any stage of her carrying the baby."

"Anytime?" Harris nodded at Oakley. "Christ, that's the most horrible thing I've ever heard. What was she supposed to do about ending a pregnancy in her last few months? I'm hoping it's not mentioned."

"It isn't. Ricky told me it was really too bad they didn't say how it was to happen. That would be premeditated murder without having to go to court. As it is now, they're in deep shit for even mentioning it. But as I said, anything done to them will need to be before a jury of their peers."

"They told me verbally what I had to do." Harris looked at Lach when she spoke to them. "Rita explained to me how she would shove me down a flight of stairs to help me out. Also, she said I could pretend to get robbed sometime, and they'd make sure the baby was murdered. She didn't actually say murder, but it wasn't hard to figure out."

"How are you feeling, honey?" Grandda hugged her hand to his cheek before speaking again. "You don't have to worry about a darn thing with them. I've got you covered. I'm a pretty well-connected man, and I've got people helping us out, so you're not harmed by them."

"I'm in some pain, but not nearly as badly as I was." Lach looked at Oakley. "You worked your miracle on my back, didn't you? Now that it feels better, I think I can finally lay on my back for a little while."

The staff had been coming into the room for Lach several times a day, not only to check on the dressing but to roll her from her left side to her right, then back the other way the next time. Harris wondered how much of her back Oakley had fixed for her, and was happy he'd not completely healed her. It wouldn't play well with anyone outside the hospital. Healing too quickly would be just as bad. Her family would call her a liar even though there were records to say how badly she'd been hurt.

"I couldn't stand to see you in pain. It was help you or go out and hunt down the people that were making you cry. I thought you'd like this so much better than me being in jail for murdering someone. Though if anyone had met your family, they'd think it was justified." Oakley laughed. "Before I forget, your dad was in. He said he'd come calling on you this evening. He was afraid you'd be too upset, and he didn't want you to stress out anymore."

Nodding, Lach looked at Harris. "Oakley told me you had a house for us. I was wondering how we could get a look at it before I'm released. At this point, I'm willing to live anywhere that will keep me safe and sound." Harris told her she'd bought it yesterday. "Oh. Well, maybe we'll be able to find another one close to you guys. I'm beginning to like having you all around all the time. Even though you're kind of bitchy, even you are growing on me, Harris." All of them laughed. Harris was really beginning to enjoy this woman.

"I've purchased it for you. Don't even bother telling me I didn't have to do that. I wanted to, and it's done." Lach said she'd never say that. "Good. Also, so you know, I've taken the liberty of marrying you two. The paperwork has been filed, and the house is in both your names, as Oakley and Lachlan Marshall. Ricky, my attorney, said the way things are going for you right now, it would go better if you can show you're getting all the support you need to raise your own children. He did want me to ask you if you know whose sperm they used."

"It wasn't Roger's if that's what you mean." Harris said it was and asked her why it wasn't his. "He told me when I asked that he'd had some kind of accident as a child, and he didn't have the ability to produce anymore. I didn't bother looking into it because I was still reeling from the fact they'd fucked me over like this."

"They have, too. I don't know if you read the contract,

and that was the reason you didn't sign it or what. But there are some things in it that could mean the death of those babies, as well as yourself." Lach told her that was one of the reasons she'd not signed it. It seemed to be very one-sided. "Oh, it is at that. Like the part where if you don't have a son for them, they can demand that you try again within four weeks of the birth of the female child. That in and of itself is very dangerous. Also, they hint at the fact that if it is a girl child, you are to dispose of it. Dispose? Christ, I hate these people."

Lach looked at Oakley. "If you're okay with being married to me, I'd very much like for us to make it official. Or at least real. I know we don't know each other all that well, but like the rest of the family, you're starting to grow on me. I kind of like you." Oakley started to answer, and Lach put up her hand. "I want you to think about this. If you take me on, I'm going to fight tooth and nail to keep these babies. They're half mine, so I'm not going to allow anyone, including you, to dispose of or harm them in any way whatsoever. Just think on that. All right?"

"I don't need to think on it, love. I want the three of you so badly I'm not sure I'm containing myself all that well." Harris was glad to hear them say that. Glad, too, that Oakley was so happy about being a father to someone else's children. "If Harris can arrange it, we'll get my family in here, and your dad, and we'll marry today. I love you so much."

Harris didn't bother with seeing if they were serious.

She called her office again and had Gilbert get a license ready for Oakley and Lach, as well as arrange for a clergyman to come and do the ceremony. Things, as far as she was concerned, were moving in the direction that would keep the children safe and make them Marshalls.

"I would also like to suggest that Oakley changes you as soon as the babies are born, Lach. Not just to be able to protect yourself, but the doctor I was speaking to said the longer they wait for your head to heal, the more chances there are that you could get an infection from it. They're not too worried right now as the swelling isn't there, but there is more of a chance of it when you leave here. They're as concerned for your welfare as they are for the babies' once you're out of here.." Lach asked her if they could do it while she was in the hospital in case something went wrong. "I've spoken to the other shifters I know, and they think you should wait for the babies to be born. The stress of changing could harm all three of you. The doctor said you needed to avoid stress."

Oakley said he had to make some arrangements for the wedding and asked if she'd stay there with Lach. Grandda was willing to hang around when she told him she had to go into work early this morning to take care of some things she had going on.

Grandda would die protecting any one of them. He was also someone that could keep Lach's mind on the day and not what had happened to her yesterday. Harris knew the man was more connected than the family gave him credit for. He'd been great friends with the ex-president's wife and had helped a great deal with some of the shit that had gone down with that. But Harris had a single favor to ask of him first.

"I'd feel much better if you were to have a gun on you, Grandda." Instead of him saying yay or nay, Lach spoke up, saying she would take it. "Are you comfortable with having it on you?"

"I'm registered to carry a gun, yes. I've taken all kinds of classes as well." Lach grinned at her. "If you're going to ask me, I don't know if I could shoot someone. But if it was between them and us living, they're going to die. I promise you that if I have to, I will do what is necessary to save Grandda's and my life."

"All right. Then you can have this." Lach took the gun from her, and Harris was impressed that she not only made sure there was one in the chamber, but that the clip was full as well. "You know what to do if you're attacked?"

"Aim for the chest, it's a bigger target. Anyplace else, and they'll still be able to come at you." Harris said that was great, but not what she meant. "Oh. Sorry. I was trying to impress you."

"You already had. But I meant that you could reach any one of us by reaching out with your mind. As soon as you feel danger, you just think of all or any of us, and we'll be here as soon as we can." Lach nodded, but Harris wondered if she understood. "I'm sure Grandda here can get you up to date on how to be a jaguar. Some of it you might not want to know."

They were both laughing when she left. Her men were planted all over the hospital. Not just for Lach, but in the event, someone came in gunning for her. Harris thought again how impressed she was with the other woman, and couldn't wait to see her outside of this place. The sooner, the better, she thought.

Chapter 4

Rebecca hung up the phone. She was royally pissed off that no one would transfer her to her daughter's room. Who would do that? she wondered. Then she thought of the man that had been hogging all the time with Lach.

"Did you get through?" Rebecca said she didn't know the code word or whatever. "Yes, that's the reason I've not been able to reach her. We have to make plans for the termination of that pregnancy. I will not allow her to ruin my life by having a little girl. Who the hell does she think she is anyway?"

While Rebecca didn't understand the reasons for not wanting a female child, she thought her daughter should be able to make that choice. It wasn't as if she wasn't going to reimburse Lach for all her time. There were rules in the contract, and Lach should have been aware of them.

"I wish she had signed that thing. Every time I think

about her refusing to sign, I want to beat her. That's what's wrong with her, you know. I didn't whip her enough as a child. Now she's gotten all uppity." Rita said she didn't think it would have done her any good. She was born that way. "I guess you're right. I do wonder how the hell she got in touch with her father. I told him to stay out of our lives. Do you suppose she's been talking to him all this time? That might not bode well for you if she has been."

"Lach did mention I'd had that child as a kid. I'm gladder every day that you convinced me to get rid of it. The thing would have messed up my life terribly had I kept it like Dad wanted me too." Rita shivered. "Roger told me it was good to know I'm being so helpful for him. Bringing a female into our home is not ever going to happen."

"Why? Why do you not want a female child, Rita? It has to be more than you just not wanting to raise a girl. Tell your mother." Rita looked around, which in turn made Rebecca look around too. They were the only people in the room. Who did she think was going to overhear them? "Tell me."

"It's Roger." Rebecca nodded. "He was accused of having sex with a baby girl when he was a teenager. He didn't, of course, but if he has one in the house, a little girl, he's afraid he will be called out again. Roger said he'd not want anything like that to happen to anyone. So, I promised him we'd only have male children. That should keep people at bay."

Rebecca sat back on the couch. Roger was a pedophile? To her way of thinking, there had to be some merit to someone accusing him of being a person who would have sex with children. And she did wonder if Rita understood it didn't have to be little girls, but any child. However, she didn't say anything about it to Rita. She was upset enough.

"You understand now, don't you, Mother?" Nodding, instead of opening her mouth to let all her questions fly, she smiled at her daughter. "We don't even go to parties where there might be little girls. I have to watch him all the time now as it is. I don't want him tempted any more than I can help it."

"Yes, yes, I can understand that." She looked around the room to give herself time to think. Rebecca wondered if there was any way that she could contact someone to find out the circumstances around the supposed allegations regarding Roger. "What are your plans concerning Lach? I'm sure you have a long list of things to get worked on."

"Not really. Roger is going to take care of it for me. He said he knows someone who can make sure Lach doesn't have the babies. Roger thinks it would be just as good if we end the pregnancy of both of the babies. That way, in a couple of weeks, we can pick and choose a better person to carry a son. One that wouldn't mind cooperating on just having a son for me." Rebecca stood up, her mind too messy for her to reason out any sort of questions. "Where are you going, Mother? I've come all this way to spend the day with you, and you look like you're going to bolt. Am I not entertaining enough for you today?"

"I have another blasted headache." She did too. It had been way too long since Rebecca had thought of anything beyond what her next party was going to be about, or what to have at it. Party planning was much easier than talking about this with Rita. "I think I might have to take a pill and lie down for a little while. You're welcome to stay, Rita, but I do need to lie down for just a bit. No more than half an hour."

"All right. I'm going to use your computer. I've been dying to look over the fashions that are in the stores now for Christmas. Have you decided on a theme for the house yet?" Rebecca said she'd not thought that far ahead with all this going on with Lach. "Yes, I know what you mean. She's always and forever messing up our plans. I'm glad now I didn't have the nursery done up. There is nothing satisfying about a nursery being done when your own sister fucks that up for you."

Rebecca made it up to her room just in time. Throwing up what she'd had on her belly wasn't how she wanted to rest. Being ill with the worry about Roger and what it had meant for him to have been in trouble bothered her enough that she was sure he was the cause of her headache. Not that Rebecca wanted to be a grandmother at her age. But she thought that, as Rita and Roger lived across town, they'd not be bringing it over all that much. She did not want a sticky, messy baby in her lovely home.

Instead of lying down, Rebecca locked her door and picked up her cell phone. She rarely used it. She didn't want to be pestered with calls when she was out. It was only in her bedroom because she'd been worried someone would break into the house and she'd not have any way to call the police. She'd read all kinds of stories where robbers would cut the lines to the house so that you'd be plunged into darkness and without a house phone.

Trying to think who she could call that would have the information she needed; the only person she could think of was her ex-husband. Frank had forever been one that would have information at the drop of a hat. She didn't figure this would be any different. Looking up his phone number had her calling him before she changed her mind. When he answered, she wasn't sure this was such a good idea, but she needed someone to answer her questions.

"It's Rebecca." He didn't say anything for several seconds. "I have a problem. Or maybe not a problem, but something that is worrying me. You seem to have all the answers, and I need you to have them now."

"Tell me what is wrong, Rebecca." She could hear that he'd put her on speakerphone and asked him about it. "I'm trying to find my wallet. I'm sure it's in my office, so I'm going to continue looking while you talk. I promise you, I'm listening."

"Roger is a pedophile." Silence. She didn't even hear any more shuffling around. "I might be mistaken about this, but I just can't think beyond what Rita just told me. She said the reason she only wants a boy is because long ago, when he was a teenager, Roger was in trouble for having sex with a little girl child. I don't know what to do. What if she's wrong and he wants to have sex with boy babies too? I know we're not on the best of terms, Frank, but I don't know what else to do. Rita is in my living room right now, thinking she's doing the right thing by killing both babies of Lach so they can start over with someone else. I'm terrified as to what that will mean for any child they have."

"Do you think that means he will have Lach killed too?" She asked him if he'd heard what she'd said. "I did. But somewhere in that line of speaking, you mentioned that Roger was going to kill off both our grandchildren. And I'm assuming Lach too. Does that bother you at all."

"You're missing the point, Frank. Just like you always do. I'm talking about Roger. Why would it matter if Lach were a victim too? There are laws about having sex with babies." He told her there were laws about killing people. "I knew it was going to be a mistake asking you for help. You can only ever focus on one thing when I'm talking to you. Nothing to do with what I want, but everything else."

"All right, for now, we'll table the fact that you're all right with having your own daughter killed to make the other one happy. When the two of them were first going together, I had him investigated. I know I wasn't living there at the time, but they're still my children. In my research, I didn't even find that a Roger Underwood existed. But that didn't stop me from having someone look a good deal deeper." Rebecca asked him what that meant. "I'm not sure, really. But it wasn't until a week or so before he and Rita started making wedding plans that I found someone with the name and social security number of a man named the same who died some fifty years ago."

"I don't understand what that has to do with him being a pedophile. You're not making any sense at all right now." He explained where he was going with this line of thought. "You think he took this dead man's name and number to hide from the fact of what he is? I guess that could be it. What other reason would he have to change himself around? I'm sure there are plenty of them, but I believe you might be right about this. How do I figure out his real name? Without him having any idea that I care."

"That's a good plan, Rebecca. If he wanted to change himself around, as you said, then he'd be pissed off if you were to start calling him by his given name. If he's willing to kill three people over having a son, then killing you wouldn't even be a blip on his radar." She told him she didn't think he was being all that nice. "I'm just stating facts to you, Rebecca. You should be worried about him."

As much as she hated to agree with Frank on anything, she had to think he was right on Roger killing her. There had to be a way for her to figure out what had really happened so her daughter wouldn't be dragged down when and if it came out. Because as surely as she was thinking about this mess, she knew Roger had a violent temper when he was pushed too hard.

"I have a couple of friends I can speak to about this, Rebecca. I would suggest, simply because you're close to him and Rita, that you let me see what I can find. I'll be able to call you at this number, won't I?" She told him it was her private cell phone number that not even Rita had. But that he had to call in the evening, after ten, as that was the only time she was near the phone. "All right. I can do that. But please, I can't say this to you enough, don't confront him. While I don't know what is going on with him, you don't want to end up on the wrong end of a bullet because you found out things you shouldn't have."

"What a terrible thing to say to me. Have you no tact, Frank?" He told her he was still just telling her facts. "I think you could have said it differently than I'd be dead. My goodness."

She hung up on him and sat there on the side of the bed. While she didn't want to admit it, Frank was more than likely right about staying away from Roger. It was going to be difficult to do, she thought since

Rita and Roger were at her home every night of the week nowadays. Rebecca looked around the room for something to distract her for a moment so that she could think. Then she spied her luggage.

A cruise. She wanted to stay away from the two of them right now, and she thought really getting away would be just the ticket. Calling the travel agency she had used before, Rebecca was glad that Barbara remembered her and had a wonderful trip she could take today, should she want to.

"Perfect." Rebecca realized she should have asked her where she was going, but thought getting out of town had to happen today. Tossing her clothing into her suitcase, she knew this was the best step right now. Getting away. Whatever she didn't have with her when she arrived on the ship, she'd just buy it. Rita would have to deal with things on her own for a change.

Calling for Meggie to help her, Rebecca told her the travel agency had called, and they had a special trip for her. Going down the stairs, having put the cell phone in her pocket, she was smiling as she entered the living room where she had left Rita. Rebecca was dismayed to find Roger there with her, and they looked as if they'd been arguing.

"Mother, I thought you were going to lie down." She told her that Barbara had called her and said she had a deal for her. "You're going on a trip? Now? But I'm having issues with Lach right now. I forbid you leaving me right now."

"You forbid me? Rita, I'm sure you're aware of this, but I'm the mother here, not you. I'm going on this trip that I've been thinking about a great deal of late. After all the stress of the last few days with Lach being in the hospital and then your father showing up, I couldn't think of a better time to get away." Rita said she wanted her to cancel her plans. "I'm not going to do that, darling. I've already paid for the ticket, and I'm to be there in an hour. I can't believe you'd even ask me to do that."

"Rita, why don't you go with your mother?" Rebecca wanted to stomp her foot and yell that she wanted this on her own. "It will be better for you both if you're not around when I have to deal with Lach. No one can say you were a part of it if you're on board a ship. I might even join you when this is finished." Roger looked right at her as he continued. "You never know what might happen if you don't go with your mother."

A threat. As surely as she didn't want her daughter to go, Rebecca knew if she didn't go, Rita would be dead before she returned. Instead of asking questions, she took the advice of Frank and didn't do anything but beg her daughter to come along with her. In the end, Rebecca thought, she'd be able to save one of her children from the monster in her home.

~*~

Oakley was helping out by looking at newspapers across the country for someone that had been accused of raping a child. He didn't have much to go on, just that it happened about ten years ago and that it had been a little girl. Looking over at Lach, he asked her how she was doing.

"I don't know. I mean, my mind keeps drifting back to the fact that Mom called Dad for help. I know she has attorneys that could have helped her with that." Oakley told her she might not trust them not to go to Roger. "I guess that could be right. Hell of a wedding day, isn't it?"

"Hey, so long as by the end of the day, I'm going to be your spouse, I don't care what I have to do in the beginning." Oakley felt his cat claw at his skin when someone knocked at the door. "I'll get it. Just stay there."

Opening the door, Oakley was relieved to find one of the agents that Shep had introduced him to before he left. They were taking no chances with anything right now. Tomorrow Lach was going to go home with him, and they were going to have staff handpicked by Harris there as well. Oakley didn't want anything to happen to his new family and was glad for the extra protection.

"Sir, Agent Harris wanted to let you and your wife know that her mother and sister have just boarded a ship for the Cayman Islands. The trip is for two weeks." Nodding, Oakley asked about Roger. "She didn't let me know what to tell you about that. I would call her if you would like more clarification."

"I will." When the door closed again, he turned the

lock. It wasn't something normally done in a hospital setting, patients with locks on their doors, but he'd installed it as soon as he returned from getting a ring for Lach. He told Lach what was going on.

"I wonder why she'd pick now to— So they'd not be around when someone tries to kill me. I don't know if I should be hurt about that or not. No one asked me to go on a cruise with them." Oakley told her he'd take her anywhere she wanted to go as soon as she was healthy enough. "I'm going to hold you to that. I've never been on a— Oakley, there is another ghost in here."

He wasn't bothered by it as much as he was the first couple of times it had happened. They only wanted her to notify someone that they were dead, then they went away. He'd only been calling Harris about the dead, and she handled it in her own way. Oakley didn't want to know details; he just moved them along after Lach gave him the details.

"She said she's been looking for someone to help her for a very long time." Oakley pulled out a pen and paper to make notes. "I'm so happy you write it down. I'm having trouble adjusting to what I'm doing about this."

"You're doing a good job. I'm sure the dead really appreciate what it is you're helping them with." He couldn't see the ghosts. Oakley wasn't sure why, and he didn't want to look into it all that deeply. Asking the first question they'd decided was the most helpful, he was waiting when he realized Lach was very quiet. "What is it, honey?"

"She doesn't remember her name. She told me she's been gone for a great many years." Lach went back to listening to the otherworldly woman. "I'm to tell you that you're not going to be able to see the ghosts like I am. That is not what they wanted to make it work. There are others, she told me, that will need your help and that of your family."

Oakley asked her what the ghost needed. Lach told him she was still talking to her. So he watched Lach while she spoke to the ghost, and wondered what the ghost meant when she said the family would help others. While Lach got the information she needed, he looked over the newspaper in front of him.

"I'm to tell you that it's her." Oakley asked what she meant. "The article you're reading, she said it's about her. She wants you to know you know who killed her. Do you?"

"Hang on. Let me see what I have here." Oakley had only been skimming the articles before, but this time he read it. "Honey, I think this is what we've been looking for. It's about a man who kidnapped a little girl from her home. She was only six weeks old."

"This is a woman here with me. I don't understand." Lach asked the woman what she meant about being the child in the article. "She said she's her mother. That when her daughter was taken, she was murdered at the same time. What's her name in the article, Oakley?"

"Marie Danielson. Her daughter was Beth." Lach repeated it to the woman and then told him that it was her. "It says she lived alone except for her child, and that someone broke into her home and killed her and took her daughter. Beth was found a week later."

He couldn't make himself say the rest. He turned and looked at Lach, and she seemed to understand. After repeating what he'd told her to Marie, Lach started to cry. He went to her and held her to him as she told him what she'd found out from Marie.

"It was Roger. But that wasn't his name. She described him to me, and it's him. His real name is Collin Carter. He had been dating her, Marie said. But she was a little uneasy about the amount of time he spent with her little girl. He'd not done anything to her then, but after a couple more dates, she cut it off with him. The next day he came into her home and killed her by strangulation. She found her little girl before the police did, and knew exactly what he'd done to her." Lach started sobbing, and he held her tighter. "She wants me to contact the loud woman. I'm assuming she means Harris."

Even the joke about Harris didn't keep her from being sad. He told Lach he'd contact her now, but not through their link. He just couldn't say those things in his connection with her. He didn't get up off the bed as he reached for the phone and put in a direct call to Harris's phone. When she answered, he almost hung up. She sounded to be in such a great mood, and he didn't want to take that from her.

"What is it, Oakley, that you couldn't just contact me the usual way? Do you have guests that you're trying to—?" She must have realized something was up. "What is it? What's happened?"

Oakley told her everything, even what had been done to the little girl. He was crying too as he described the scene as it was described in the newspaper. His belly was protesting too like it knew things were not as they should have been with this death.

"Is Lach all right?" He told her they were both bruised by this. "I'm sending someone to come and get you both. I don't care if she's ready to be released or not. I want you both where I can protect you. Also, we'll have everything arranged so that you can marry at the house. It'll be safer, as well as having more room."

"I'm all right with that." She gave him the code word the agent would have. Also, she was doubling the guards around them until they were home. "Harris, he did so many despicable things to that baby. He killed her like she was nothing at all."

"I'm going to get him, Oakley. I promise you. I'm going to get him before the end of the day." He told her he was going to pack Lach up, and they'd be ready. They needed to be out of here. "Yes, you do. I'm also going to send your brother with my men. I want him to be there in the event jackass comes around. Not that you couldn't protect Lach when it came to that, but I'd just as soon have too many around than not enough."

In thirty minutes, Shep was there with his grandda. Hugging them both didn't seem unmanly at all to him, but a way to draw strength and security from them. Grandda even hugged Lach like he was never going to let her go. Shep, wisely, didn't touch Oakley's mate.

It took them another hour to be on the road. Shep had to check out of the hotel they'd been staying in, and Grandda had to pick up a few snacks to eat on the way home. They all got a good laugh out of the three large bags of snacks when he finally got in the car.

"Just who are you feeding these snacks too?" Lach was seated next to him with her head on his shoulder when she was handed one of the bags. "Oh, look. I love these candy bars."

While she ate one of the chocolate bars, he spoke to his brother. He was going to a home he'd never been in, and he didn't even know where it was located. Shep was telling him what he and the others had done for the house, making sure there was a bed for them, and that the staff was all ready to start working for them.

Lach and I will have to get around to getting baby stuff too. I mean, we're having twins, and that's scary enough. Shep looked at him, and Oakley had a feeling he was trying very hard not to tell him something. *You've done it, haven't you?*

Yes. All of us went online and started shopping the moment you told us you and Lach were having twins. Oakley liked that he didn't point out they were not his children but thought of them as Marshalls already. *Consider it a wedding gift. Which, by the way, is going to be held at your home. The wedding, I mean. Frank is coming down as well to be there for his little girl.*

Thanks, Shep. You're about the best big brother anyone could have. Shep told him he knew that. *Jerk.*

By the time they pulled up in front of their new home, Lach was asleep. She hated falling asleep all the time, but Rodney told her it was a combination of being pregnant and being hurt. So now, when she needed to close her eyes, even for a little while, she no longer fought it but let herself drift off. Oakley hated to wake her, but he wanted her to go into the house first.

"Good heavens. This looks like a frigging hotel. Why is it so huge?" Grandda told Lach she was going to need more room with the babies coming along. "I do hope you'll pick out a place for you to stay so you can visit us when you want. I have a feeling I'm going to be depending on you a great deal when they come along."

Oakley didn't mention the houses on the property. He thought if Grandda did need some space of his own, he would tell him then. For now, he was glad to have him coming around when he wanted. He was sure, too, that Grandda was going to be tickled pink about the name Lach had thought of for their daughter. Alma Grace was all they knew for their daughter. The boy's name was going to be determined once they figured out some of the family names on her side of the family.

Walking through the house with Lach was fun. She loved each and every one of the rooms. She also fell in love with the master bathroom. The tub, an old fashioned one with clawed feet, was something she said she'd dreamed of all her life. He was thrilled that there seemed to be enough room in it for the two of them if they were to take a bath together. Then they ended up in the nursery for the children.

Chapter 5

Rebecca loved the open sea. Standing near the railing, she didn't care how the breeze was making her hair messy. There was nothing, not at all, for miles and miles as she looked out over the vastness of the water. She turned when she heard Rita say her name.

"Come look, Rita. This is why I love to go on cruises. There is always something to catch your imagination. The waves are beautiful this morning too." Rita didn't move, and Rebecca laughed. "Why on earth would you come on a cruise if you didn't have any plans of looking where we are?"

"Roger said I should push you over the edge of the ship." Positive that she'd heard her daughter wrong, she asked her what she'd said. "He said it's time we cashed in the policy we took out on you years ago. Roger has been planning your demise, Mother, for such a long time. It's finally going to pay off for us."

"What did you just say to me?" Rita told her again what she and Roger had planned out. How pushing her over the edge would be quick and easy for her. "I can't believe you'd go along with this, Rita. I'm your mother. The only one you have."

Rebecca held onto the railing, wrapping her other arm around the pole closest to her so she'd not be easily tipped. Rita came toward her, and at the last moment, she moved to be about ten feet from her down the rail. Rebecca had never been so frightened in all her life.

"He has such good plans about things. Making sure we're secure for when we're older. I did tell him that you were my mother, and I didn't think it was fair of him to make me kill you. But he pointed out that you're very old and won't be around much longer anyway, when he's still young and healthy. I had to make a sound choice, you see." Rita looked at her. The smile on her daughter's face was serene as if she'd not explained to her own mother that she was going to kill her. "With you and Lach gone with the children that she was carrying for us, people will feel so sorry for us. They'll invite us to parties and the like. It will open so many doors for the two of us. Besides, don't you want us to be accepted by people? Have a secure future? I'm sure you don't want either of us, Roger and I, to be without, do you?"

"I don't understand this. Rita, I've been your champion for your entire life. I can't believe you can stand there, acting like I should be agreeable to the fact that you're going to murder me." Rita said it wasn't murder. "Then what would you call it? You're going to push me over the side of this ship. That is exactly what murder is, when you take my life."

"No, Mother, you're thinking of this like it's all about you. It's not. Roger explained to me that you need to think of the two of us. Our future. Our way of life." She laughed a little. "It's not murder. Let's call it mercy. I'm being merciful by pushing you over the rail now instead of you getting too old and having to be taken care of. I'm doing you a great favor in this."

"Thanks, but I don't want you to do me any kind of favor like that. I'd rather live to be a very old woman and die in my sleep." Rita told her she couldn't allow her to do that. "Yes, you can, Rita. Don't do this. I don't know why, just because Roger told you to do it, you're willing to go along with murdering me."

Anger flashed on her face. "It's not fucking murder, I told you. Don't say that again, Mother. You're pissing me off." Rebecca apologized and told her she wouldn't say it again. "Good. I don't want us to use our last time together arguing with each other. You'd not want me to be upset whenever I think about you being gone. You're going to let me do what I need to do so I can be safe in my golden years."

Rebecca had never been so glad to see someone coming out on the deck with her as she was the couple that had. Latching onto them, telling them they had to see the ocean, Rebecca knew she sounded nutty. But her mind was frozen, it seemed, on the fact that Rita was planning to pitch her overboard.

When she was close enough to the door to slip inside, Rebecca decided she was going to stay indoors for the rest of the trip. Never going near the railing would make it so she'd not be able to toss her off. Rita joined her at the table she sat down at when she'd entered, and smiled.

"You're not going to be able to thrall me on this, Mother. There are other ways to do this for you than just the railing. It would have been easier, yes, but I'm up for whatever it takes to put you into a better place. You might as well get it over with. Don't you think?" Rebecca didn't bother answering her daughter but did raise her hand to get some help in the form of one of the waitstaff in the dining area. "I'd not mention this to anyone, Mother. I do have a gun, and I'm not afraid to kill anyone that questions me about it. You'll regret that I had to kill people when it's inevitable that you're going to do this for us anyway."

Rebecca ordered a large glass of wine. Then changing her mind, she asked for a bourbon neat. When it was delivered to her, she noticed her hands were shaking so hard she nearly sloshed every bit of it out on the tablecloth. Setting the glass down, she looked at her daughter with new eyes.

"You of all people I'd never have expected to be crazy." Rita slammed her hands down on the table and told her she wasn't crazy, just very smart. "Call it what you want, child, but planning the demise of your own mother, not to mention your own sister, isn't sane. What makes you think you'll be able to get away with this? Or that someone isn't going to notice you tipping me off the decking?"

The smile again. It wasn't a new smile or even one that Rebecca hadn't seen on her daughter's face all her life. But now, knowing what sorts of things were going through her mind, Rebecca knew Rita had been insane her entire life. Rebecca had just chosen to ignore the telltale signs because whatever made Rita happy made her happy as well.

She had another drink and realized as she was about to order a third that if she were drunk, her murder would be much easier for Rita to make happen. What she wouldn't give to be able to talk to someone that might believe her. Then her mind latched on that woman, Harris. The friend of her sane daughter.

When lunch was ready to be served, Rebecca had a plan. Not a well thought out one, but a plan all the same. She had a feeling Rita wasn't going to be easy to get rid of now that she was ready to do her job. Rebecca let out a little laugh and knew she sounded manic. Reaching the woman was the only way she could think of to come out of this without being killed.

For the rest of the day, and into the evening, Rita followed her around. Rebecca didn't go out on the deck at all, and she hated that. It was what she loved most about a long cruise. Well, she used to. Now she wondered if she'd want to do anything near the open seas again. Rita had ruined that for her.

When nightfall was coming on, Rebecca decided to have a lavish meal. It might be her last, she told herself and dismissed that thought right away. Dressing up in her cabin was the only time she was able to pull out her cell phone and make a call to Frank. At the last moment, she decided that texting him might be safer for her.

Rita is going to kill me. Like it's nothing at all to throw me from the ship. Roger is going to kill Lach and the babies as well. For their future, she told me. Rebecca gave him the name of the ship and all the information on her itinerary. *Frank, please send me some help. Rita is insane. I've never noticed that before today.*

When he answered her, Rebecca was so happy her phone had been turned to silent that she sobbed a little. She had to read the message twice before she finally felt like she might just make it off this thing without being in a body bag when they landed.

We're looking for Roger, but he's disappeared. Lach is in good hands and safe. The door to her cabin was locked behind her, and she was glad she'd not shared a room with Rita as she had wanted. Now she knew why. *Harris is going to get to you. I'm not sure how that is going to work or when, but she said soon. Also, here is her number if you need anything right now.*

Thank you. Thank you both so much. Rita has a gun, and she told me if I were to tell anyone what she's said to me, she'll kill them. Thinking of anything else she should tell him, Rebecca knew she wasn't out of the woods with Rita just yet. She still had to stay safe until help arrived. *Frank, I have been so terrible to you. I'm so sorry.*

Harris said to act normal and to not be alone with Rita if you can. She also said for you to not go anywhere you might be cornered. She cried again. Frank, her ex-husband, was helping her even after all she'd done to him. *Rebecca, we're going to have to talk when you get back here. About a lot of things.*

Yes. Someone knocked on her door, and Rebecca knew it had to be Rita. *Rita and I are going to dinner now. I'll talk to you about anything you wish. Please be careful around Roger. They're both insane.*

Rebecca nearly put her phone in her small purse but decided that was just buying trouble. Instead, she put it in the safe in her room with her other things. If Rita were to have found her phone, she was sure she'd just flat out kill her instead of following through with whatever her plans were now. Going to the door, she smiled at her daughter and told her she was ready to go.

"You don't want to just sit a little bit?" Alarms were going off in her mind. Cornered. She'd be cornered. Rebecca said she was very hungry and moved out of her room completely and into the hall, locking the door behind her. "Mother, it's going to happen sooner or later.

Why would you want to have it put off? You'll never sleep well, wondering when I'm going to have to help you along."

"I'd rather it never happened at all, Rita." She moved down the hallway to the dining room. "I'm not going to go easily, either. You should remember that, while I might be old in your eyes, I'm a spry woman who works out daily."

"And I'm a younger woman who has been planning this for a long time. I will win in the end, Mother. I can't believe how selfish you are to think of only yourself in this. I would have thought you'd be happy that Roger and I are so forward thinking." Rebecca told her it involved her murder. Rita grabbed her arm and pinched hard into her skin. "I told you it's not murder, Mother. Don't say that to me again."

Her arm was going to be bruised, Rebecca thought. Even as she looked at it after she was released, she could see that Rita had drawn blood, both on the top of her arm where her fingers had been and under, where her thumbnail had dug deeply into her skin. Taking a tissue from her purse, Rebecca was startled when Rita jerked the purse from her.

"Good girl, Mother. No cell phone. I'd really hate to think you went ahead and contacted someone about this. It will only make it harder when I have to make sure no one knows about what we've discussed." Rita laughed again. It was beginning to freak her out now. "I was speaking to Roger before I went to get you, and he said if you were to tell someone, he'd be happy for me to make it look like you were crazy and that you jumped over on your own. Isn't that a delicious idea?"

Not bothering with answering Rita, she moved on into the dining room and asked for a table. If Rita joined her or not, she was going to sit down and have a wonderful meal, ordered off the menu instead of getting in line for the buffet. She didn't put it past Rita to poison her food now. Everything she ate or drank wasn't going to be out of her site from now on.

After dinner, Rebecca sat at her table enjoying the show until everything was finished. The meal was perfection, she supposed. Rebecca hadn't been able to enjoy much of it because she was terrified she'd be drugged or poisoned. Rita kept up a steady conversation with her, but Rebecca didn't bother engaging in any of it. She had to keep herself alert and ready to save her life.

Going back to her room, Rebecca made sure she moved down the hallway with other groups. When her door came up, she slipped in and locked the door behind her quickly. Rita was laughing on the other side of her door when she turned on the lights. Fear of Roger coming out of a corner or even the bathroom had her picking up the umbrella by the door and holding it like a weapon until she was sure she was alone.

Sitting on the couch, Rebecca didn't know how much longer she could do this. It wasn't just scary, but it was playing havoc with her nerves as well. Wondering how men and women did this sort of thing on death row, she had a great deal more respect for the people that worked there. Being high strung all the time wasn't good on your heart either, she supposed.

~*~

Oakley heard something in the kitchen and picked up the gun he'd been left as he moved in that direction. Lach was resting on the couch they'd gotten yesterday, and he'd been working at his computer. Well, he'd been looking at his computer, not getting too much done. He was a married man now, thanks to his family, and he couldn't be happier. Sliding into the room, not making a sound, he nearly hit his brother Heath in the head when he turned and looked at him over the refrigerator door.

"Are you trying to give me a heart attack?" Heath told him he was getting a drink. "You might well have gotten yourself shot by not making yourself known to me. Damn it, Heath, there's a madman out there looking to kill off my wife and children. Don't do that again."

"I'll be more careful. I actually thought you and Lach would be making dinner about now. I don't have much in the way of food in my place, and I wanted to bum a meal off you." Lach came into the kitchen and kissed him on the cheek and touched her hand to Heath's back as she made her way to the oven. It didn't bother his cat so much when she did that. Her hugging his younger brothers drove him insane. "Are you going to invite me to dinner, Lach? I'm wasting away here, and Oakley said I can't eat with you."

"I did not. He's lying." Both Heath and Lach laughed. "I guess I fell right into that one, didn't I? Lach put on a roast earlier today so we could eat when we wanted. It's been hard for me to get her to rest when she's supposed to. But I'm getting the hang of telling her I've got it. We'll need a cook soon, so she doesn't scare me to death all the time. But the roast? I've been salivating all day when the aroma trailed down the hall to me."

"I was going into town, taking a little walk, when I could smell it. Christ, I'd eat here nightly if I weren't so afraid you'd poison me to get me to stop." Lach was starting to pull the roast out of the oven, but Heath moved her away so he could do it. "You need to be taking advantage of all this male help around you, darling. It won't be that long before you aren't able to bend over so well."

"What a charmer you are. And you want to eat with us?" Heath asked her what he'd said that was wrong. "You called me fat, dumbass. And mentioned that I'm going to get bigger. Not a way to get food in your belly. Just putting that out there."

The lid was taken off the roaster, and both he and Heath moaned. The sucker was big—they'd cooked one this size so they could have leftovers. He didn't want Heath to stay, because that would mean fewer open-faced roast beef sandwiches later in the week.

"Did you know Shep is all alone in his house? I guess Harris took off sometime last night for a job." Oakley knew where she was going and why, but he didn't mention it to Heath. "Shep would really like to be invited to dinner too, I'm betting."

Before he could tell his brother to shut up, him being there was more than he wanted, Lach told him to call them all over for food. They had more than enough. Oakley stomped to his office again, not wanting to hear about how many people were coming now.

His phone was ringing when he sat down. Having a house phone was all right, he supposed. Neither he nor Lach had given the number out to too many people. It was going to be for people that didn't know them all that well. Also, to order food in. The cell phone he had was nice, but he thought it was difficult to get away from people bothering him all the time if he had to carry it around. All he wanted to do was spend time with Lach.

Picking up the phone, he listened to the person on the other end of it talking to someone. Oakley thought the second person was his dad, but he couldn't tell when the man that called started talking to him.

"Oakley, I'm here with your grandfather. He's has had an accident and needs someone to come and pick him up. He's not been injured too badly but has refused to go to the hospital. Would it be convenient for you to come and pick him up?" Oakley reached out for his grandda instead of answering the man right away. "He's a really all right guy, isn't he?"

"He's the best there is." Grandda answered him, and Oakley asked him if he'd been in an accident. Grandda laughed and said he was at Dean's home playing with Dru, their son. "Mr.... I'm sorry, I didn't catch your name. Who is this I'm talking to again?"

"Oh, sorry. Ben Smith." Oakley told him he'd come and get his grandda if he just told him where he was. "We're on Rat Cove Lane down by the river. I'm happy you're coming, Oakley. He sure is a pistol."

"Yes, he is. A little slower moving around now that he's contending with a hip replacement." Mr. Smith said he didn't seem to be diminished that much, but he was up there in age. "Try slowing him down. He's worse than a toddler at times."

Oakley knew his grandda would be pissed off if he'd heard the man talking to him. Knowing for a fact that the man didn't have his grandda made him feel better. Also, he knew he didn't know much about him if he thought Grandda had a broken hip, much less a hip replacement. His grandda was as spry as anyone he knew, including himself. Oakley told the man he'd be there in twenty minutes. After hanging up, he called all his family to let them know what was going on.

Well, if that don't beat all. I'm not anywhere near Rat Cove. Durn people. What do you suppose he's thinking to do by telling you that? Oakley told him what he thought. *Oh. Oh, my goodness, I didn't think of that. I'm sure glad you knew it. What's he thinking? That he'd get you and then make Lach do something stupid? I wonder if he knows how smart your little wife is about things. Or you, for that matter.*

He could also be waiting, hoping you leave the house soon and leave Lach there all alone. I haven't the mind of Harris, but that's what I'd think. Shep was probably righter than he was about getting him alone. *I have an idea. I know Heath is at your house — he told me about dinner tonight. Why don't you leave there and leave Heath to protect Lach?*

Or a better idea would be for Oakley to stay here, and I pretend to be going to get Grandda. I think I'd live longer if I didn't have to be alone with Oakley's wife. Oakley laughed, but did agree with his brother. *I think I've pushed him about as far as I can with inviting you all to dinner. With Lach's permission, but you guys all know how Oakley loves his leftovers when it comes to having a fat open-faced sandwich.*

I think I like that one too. Shep said he loved it and felt better about it. Then he asked everyone if they thought Heath going to the spot was good thinking. Everyone agreed. Shep also had some advice for both him and Heath. *Don't be a hero by thinking you can take him in alive. Once you get there or he attacks, then kill him. I don't care if he faces a jury or not; I'm going to be just as satisfied if he's no longer a part of our lives.*

Heath borrowed Oakley's keys and went out to his truck. While they didn't have any idea what was going to happen next, Shep said he'd be close by to help, as did Rodney and Grandda. Everyone was in place as they waited for whatever was going to happen to happen.

By the way, I left the front door ajar. Oakley asked him why he'd do something like that with a killer on the loose. *Because he couldn't have been looking at the back of the house, or he would have known I was there. So, he'll come into the house all sneaky like, and you can control where he is when you have to kill him. I don't know a lot about stealth work, but I'd think that getting caught in the kitchen with a killer would be the worst kind of place. Too tight. At least the hall and dining room affords you more room to attack.*

Oh. They were all laughing now, and Oakley held onto Lach as he told her what was going on. "So, I need for you to pretend, just for a moment, that you're here alone. Don't be afraid, love. He's not going to be close enough to breathe on you, much less try and kill you."

"I know that silly."

She made her way to the dining room with him hot on her heels. As soon as they entered the dining room, they watched Roger come into the house by looking at his reflection in one of the china cabinets in that room.

He was armed with a small handgun, and it looked as if he had several knives in the back of his pants. Oakley nearly screamed when Lach spoke. He was so tense, he thought he would have screamed had he not been just ready to shift to his cat.

"Honey, is that you? I thought you'd be gone a good deal longer." The small laughter from Roger made Oakley pissed. He was acting just like him. Or trying to.

"Oakley? Did you remember to get some milk?"

Lach moved to stand in the doorway just as Roger was coming around the dining room table. There wasn't any way Roger had missed her standing there. It was confirmed when she backed up, saying Roger's name then asking him what he was doing there.

"I've come to make sure you've done just what my wife told you to do. To get rid of the girl child." Lach told him she wasn't going to do that. "I thought you'd say that. Stubborn to the very end, aren't you, Lach? Well, I've come here to make sure you're no longer a threat to Rita and myself. Killing you will give me great pleasure. Just knowing you're out of the way means we can live our life any way we wish without having to worry about you coming in behind us and messing up our little lies."

"You mean like the one you told my sister about you not being the one who raped that baby, Roger? Or killed her mother? Perhaps you'd have more memories about what you've done if I were to call you by your real name— Collin Carter. Isn't that right?" He asked her where she'd found that. "Oh, there is plenty of information to be found if you have the right people working with you— like my sister-in-law, Harrison. You might not know this about her, but she's very good at making people regret messing with her family. I don't suppose you've heard from Rita today, have you? I would get on that if I were you. You don't want to miss talking to each other one more time, do you?"

"What are you fucking talking about?" Lach was taunting Roger. While Oakley didn't know why he had a feeling, she was doing this with the blessing of Harris. Staying where he was out of sight, for now, he heard the hum of something he'd not noticed before. "You have no idea what the hell you're talking about. My wife and your mother are on a cruise ship that will be coming back soon. Well, at least my wife is coming home."

He found the source of the humming and stared at the device in the corner of the room for a little longer before he realized what he was looking at. A camera, if he didn't miss his bet. He also figured the sucker was recording all the sounds going on as well.

"I don't think you're thinking about the whole picture here, Collin. Let me give you some clues. I just love clue games. I'm sure you can guess what I'm referring to before I have to give you too many clues." He told her to shut up. "The first clue is, why do you think I was left here in my home when we all knew you didn't have Grandda? Come on. You can answer it. I know you can."

"You're not alone." Lach laughed and yelled *bingo* to him. "And how do you think that is possible when I saw your husband, or whatever he is to you, leaving? Riddle me that, Lach."

"Someone did leave here, Collin." He told her his name was Roger. "No, it's not. I mean, I'm not even sure that Collin is your real name. Is it? Well, not that it matters. But I would like you to meet my husband. And we are married, jackass."

He moved from behind the dining room table and stood near Lach. When she reached down and scratched him behind the ears, he purred to her. Whatever Lach had going on, he was going to have to pay attention. Nothing was going to happen to her as long as he was around.

"Christ. Is that even real? Probably not. What is it about women that they think having a little plaything around is going to stop me from killing them? I'm a pro at this, Lach. Dogs and shit like them don't bother me. You've just signed his death warrant too if you want to know the truth. As soon as my wife returns, she'll be joining you on the other side." He pretended to think about it. "Or she could be in hell. She's not even close to being sane. Did you know that? Your sister is off her rocker. More so than people think I am."

When he pointed his gun at her, Lach didn't move. The only thing that alerted him to her fear was that she pulled tightly at his fur. As soon as Collin smiled at Lach, Oakley felt his cat's rage, and he leapt at the other man.

The taste of blood filled his mouth. It was dark with madness, something he'd never had the occasion to taste before, but he knew instinctively what it was. Collin, or whatever his name happened to be, was as mad as anyone he'd ever encountered before. But he would soon be out of their lives forever.

Chapter 6

Harris moved into the bedroom and put her gun to the head of the woman lying in the large bed. As soon as Rebecca opened her eyes, wide with fear, Harris told her not to scream. Not only did she obey her, but Rebecca also put both her hands up and told her there was a gun under her pillow.

"A fat lot of good it's doing you when I was able to get the drop on you." Harris turned on the light, filling the room with shadows and lights. "Don't get dressed, but come into the living room. I need you to look as normal as possible for the next few hours."

Harris went into the living room and sat down on one of the nice chairs. She was going to have to talk Shep into taking a cruise with her. She'd forgotten how nice they were. When Rebecca joined her, she told her to have a seat. She didn't argue with her, as she had hoped she would, but sat and kept her mouth shut.

"Your son-in-law is dead." Whatever reaction she thought she'd get with that statement wasn't Rebecca falling over sobbing and thanking her. "I didn't do it, but Oakley and Lach did. His obit is going to say he died in a horrific car accident rather than having anyone think he might well have been killed. I'm not going to give you any more information than that. I also warn you now that you'd better not be telling anyone about our midnight visit. You will end up on my shit list, and that is not a place you'd want to be. Understand?"

"I understand. However, you should know that my daughter is insane. I mean, I don't know what Frank told you, but she was going to kill me. Just toss me away as if I were nothing to her." Harris told her she more than likely wasn't anything to her. That she had her own set of rules. "Yes, I suppose you might be right. But I'm terrified of her. She was so calm about what she was telling me that it was as if she was talking about how the weather was nice out."

"I've come here to tell you I don't think you're any better than Rita. You've both treated my new sister-in-law like shit, and if it were up to me, I'd toss you off the boat myself. But it's not. So, I guess we'll have to agree that I won't kill you tonight." Rebecca looked at her with terror in her eyes. "I will, however, cut you some slack if you promise me you're never going to talk to Lach again. Also, that as soon as you can arrange it, you're to leave the state, never to return. Frank is going to be living closer to his daughter, the one that you took from him when all you ever wanted to do was hold that over his head. If I see you within a mile of the state of Ohio, you'll never know you're dead."

"Why would you say something like that to me? I've just had a horrific day, and here you sit, adding more onto it. Do you have any idea what my daughter said to me? How she was going to kill me?" Harris pointed out that she wasn't dead. "Not because of you, apparently. You'd probably have a party if I were to end up dead, wouldn't you?"

"I would, actually. A huge one that would be a wonderful occasion for a great many people. Your staff, neighbors. Even people at the grocery store wouldn't be bothered if you were to end up dead. You've been a blot on a great many people's lives that don't particularly give a shit about you." She told her she had friends. "Perhaps. More than likely, people just like you. A bitch with a little money that lords it over people until you chase them off with your rudeness. I have known a great many people like you, and fortunately, they're all pushing up daisies because I've killed them. You see, Rebecca, when you called Frank to tell me about your troubles, you had no idea that you were going to have a hitman for the United States government come to your aid. The next words out of your mouth will be the death of you if you choose wrong. Are you going to leave the state of Ohio forever?"

"Yes. Just so you know, I don't like you." Harris

laughed. "How can you live with yourself knowing you've ended the lives of people? I'm sure you're just as insane as my daughter."

"Frankly, I could care less what you think about me. Nor if you like me or not. I'm what I am because I made something of myself. You have only done the barest of work to get yourself where you wanted to be. A semi wealthy bitch without friends—or, as it turns out, a family—to call your own." She said she had Lach. "No, you don't. You aren't to have a thing to do with her. I will kill you if you come around. You'll never see your grandchildren either. No pictures of them will be sent to you. You'll not get a Christmas card from the family, nor will you ever be able to have anything to do with Lach. They're all dead to you. Or you will be. Test me on this, and as I said, you will never realize you're dead."

"Do you talk to everyone this way? It's no wonder you have to come into rooms in the middle of the night to have conversations with people." Rebecca started to stand, and Harris told her to sit. "I want to know what you're going to do about helping me out. Or have you only come here to make sure I'm put in my place?"

Almost as if the timing were perfect, someone knocked on the door. Before she went to answer it, Harris stood up to hide behind the door. She told her not to mention her or she'd simply end her life and that of the person. Pulling open the door, Rebecca pulled at her robe and asked what was going on.

"Mrs. Russell? I'm sorry to wake you in the middle of the night, but I was wondering if you could come with me. There's been an accident." Rebecca asked what sort of accident. "Would you mind coming with me, please?"

Harris slipped into the hall when she was sure Rebecca and the man were gone. Going into the room across the hall, Harris put her wet suit back on, as well as her boots and gloves. In seconds, no more than half a minute, Harris was climbing out the window and to the water below. Landing no more than a few feet from where her ride, an all-black jet ski, was, just where she'd tied it off, Harris climbed onto it and let it drift away from the ship for several minutes until she was sure no one could see her from above.

Riding back to the boat that had brought her out here, she thought about what the older woman was going to find when she got to the medical unit. No one would need to worry about Rita Underwood again. She had, as people were going to believe, killed herself in the main dining room of the large ship.

Harris had gone to the cabin Rita was supposed to be in. Not finding her there, she pulled out her phone and began searching the ship via their own camera to find where the woman had gone. Finding her in the dining room, Harris, dressed in her all-black clothing, snuck into the room to find her prey. Not only was Rita alone, but she seemed to be making notes about something.

It only took her minutes to shoot the dart into the back

of her head. It would knock her out for several minutes, long enough for Harris to not only put the poison into her drink but also to look over the notes she'd been writing. It was a suicide note, one that Harris knew was supposed to be from her mother and not Rita.

Backing away from the table, she waited for Rita to wake. She was none the wiser, it seemed, for her little nap, and she picked up her drink and drained the glass. Harris had thought it would take a lot longer for her to know Rita was dead. Most people didn't guzzle down good whiskey but sipped it over time.

As soon as Rita's head fell forward on the table, Harris moved up behind her to check her pulse. Nothing. The drug had caused her to have a massive stroke and killed her immediately, just as she'd hoped. Leaving the empty bottle of the drugs they'd find in her system on the table, Harris had made her way back to the room she had been in and changed into her regular clothing to go and talk to Rebecca.

The more she found out about the Russell family, the more she wished she'd not promised Lach that she'd not kill her mom unless necessary. She may still have to do that, but for now, she'd kept her promise to the other woman and had given Rebecca the rules. All the rules, including the one where she couldn't enter the state of Ohio again, were from Lach. The girl was quickly becoming someone Harris admired, which was a scant few people in this world.

I'm finished here. Shep told her what was going on where he was. He'd told her that Collin was dead before she'd even gotten on the first boat. *Rita was easy. She drank like a fish; did you know that?*

That must have been calming for you. You be careful. Are you coming home tonight? She said she didn't think she could. That she was exhausted and didn't feel like trying to get some sleep on a plane. *I was hoping you'd stay there. For as much as I'd like you to be home, I also don't want you too exhausted to be here safely.*

How is Lach? I was going to call her tomorrow to tell her it's finished with her sister. Shep told her she more than likely knew already. *Probably. I did just what she wanted and didn't let her suffer. Though it was very tempting to kill off her mother too. She's a bigger bitch than even I am. She had the nerve to tell me I was rude. This coming from a woman that was more than willing to have Lach abort her children.*

People are going to disappoint you all the time if you allow them to. I heard that from someone very important to me. She laughed when she realized it was her. *When you get home, I think we should tell the rest of the family you're going to have a baby. It's been weeks now, and I'm about to bust with all these others having babies. I cannot wait to see you large with our baby.*

I'm sure this suit I have on is going to not fit me quite the same again. They both laughed. She was nearing the boat when she told him where she was. *Do me a favor, will you, Shep? Will you please go over and talk to Oakley and*

Lach about this? I know she said she just wanted it over with, but I want you to make sure for me. Killing someone's sister isn't like killing a stranger. I don't want her to not want to be around me anymore. I'm enjoying having female friends I can hang out with that don't give a shit as to what I do for a living.

I'll go over first thing in the morning. I promise you. She thanked him and then asked if he thought she was silly. *No, I don't. I think you don't want anything to happen to your family, and that would include killing someone to make them safe.*

I'll feel a lot better about this as soon as I speak to her. Hopefully, she won't be upset. What happened to Collin's body? Did they pick it up on time? Also, I ordered a complete cleanup. I hope they did a good job on that as well. Shep told her he'd been taken away and that Oakley said there wasn't a speck of anything around to indicate a large jaguar had torn a man's throat out so badly it removed his head. *I hope he's not feeling guilty about this. He had to do it. Roger left him no choice at all.*

He doesn't act like it. In fact, I think they're both relieved to know Roger's out of their life. I've not spoken to her since you finished up on the ship. I'm sure she'll be just as happy with that. Not just for her sake, but for the children. That was the main reason she'd been so happy to do this. To make sure her niece and nephew were safe. *I cannot wait for us to be able to make the announcement. You've no idea how much I want to tell Grandda to be quiet about us making him a great grandda too.*

I'm coming home tonight. I need to be with you. I never realized before just now that you make me feel perfect. I know I'm far from it, but you make me feel that way. Shep told her that to him, she was perfect. *You keep that up, big boy, and you might just get lucky when I get home.*

He was laughing still when she closed the connection. Harris wanted to be home now in the worst sort of way. Going straight to the airport when they were on land again, she was on her way home in less than twenty minutes.

~*~

Lach stretched as she woke. She didn't think she'd ever slept that well in her entire life. Not only did her body feel about as relaxed as it ever had, but her mind was clear, and her skin even felt renewed. Rolling to her side, she looked at Oakley as he lay there looking at her.

"I thought for sure you were going to sleep all day again. Did you know that when you sleep, you snore so quietly it's almost cute?" She told him she did not snore. "You do. I swear. It's adorable. I mean, it's not even the least bit annoying like Shep's is. He's loud. I wonder at times how Harris stands it. Come to think of it, she might snore louder. Do you suppose that is one of the traits we get in mates—we all have the same sleeping habits?"

"I do not snore." She rolled over him and sat up over his waist. "Did you want to go to the doctor with me tomorrow? Or today. How long was I asleep?"

"Just the usual time. But we did go to bed fairly early,

so I guess about ten hours. I think having less stress is what—" She told him she didn't want to talk about her family. "I do have to tell you one thing, Lach. Before Harris comes over for dinner. She is terrified that you're going to be upset that your sister is gone as well."

"I'm not upset at all. I've been reading over the reports she found on the two of them. They were both insane. Did you read them?" He said he'd not. "Seventeen people are missing that lived around or worked for them. Seventeen people. I don't even want to think about what they might have done to these babies." She shivered and laid her head down on his chest.

"They would never have gotten them. Nor you. I promise you that." She said she knew that, but it had scared her when Roger showed up. "You, my dear, were brilliant in confronting him as you did. Shep coming up with that plan to get him to think you were here alone was also brilliant. We got him in the act, and that is better than anything in the world. I love you. So much."

"And I love you. But I don't want to talk about family anymore. I want to have you make love to me. It's been put off long enough. I know you were healing me all along with the kisses and touches. My wounds are all gone, and the one on my head is almost closed up. I'm stronger every day, and I want to have sex with you." He pulled her up for a kiss and rolled her to her back. "Yes, this is just where I wanted to be. However, with both of us naked and you deep inside of me."

"I aim to please." His hands were warm as they moved over her body. There was something so profoundly amazing about having her body touched by someone. It was even better that he loved her too. "You're right. You're way too overdressed right now. How about if I take all these off you and have a little exploratory fun with your lovely body."

There wasn't any time for her to tell him yes. Before she could even guess what he was going to do next, the sound of ripping clothing made her body wet with anticipation. Her nipples ached to be touched. Something so primal rolled over her, and she knew she wanted Oakley to bite her, to make her come with the feel of his teeth as they sank into her skin.

"Oakley, I need you." She was on fire and couldn't seem to make her mouth work to tell him what she wanted. But when he scraped his teeth, sharper than she remembered them being, over her skin, she screamed out his name as a climax took her breath away. "Again. Please? I want to come like that again."

It was like she had challenged him into seeing if he could kill her with coming. Every place he touched her, she would feel her body respond. Not in small climaxes either, but her body felt like it was going to explode with the feelings he gave her.

"Do you have any idea how much I love you, Lach? More than I can put into words. I'm showing you, showing you how much I love you by worshipping you.

All of you." She cried then, so touched by his words and actions. "I love you."

"I love you too. My heart is overflowing with my love for you."

He moved up her body. Having touched every part of her, he kissed his way up her until he got to her pussy. "I need a taste of you."

She would swear for the rest of her life that he'd stuck her toes into an electrical socket. Her throat closed off; her ears rang. Every part of her body seemed to have come apart the moment he licked her from gate to clit, only to suckle hard at her womanhood.

Lach opened her eyes, knowing for some reason that she'd fainted. It had been too much, but she'd gladly have him do it to her again. The next time, however, she'd make sure she stayed awake. She'd missed him filling her. Missed him taking her as his own. Wrapping her legs around his legs, she met him stroke for stroke as he took her hard.

"Christ, I'm so close to coming. I thought for sure I'd killed you." She said she'd thought so too. As he doubled his effort to take her to new highs to come with him, Lach dug her nails into his back and bowed up off the bed as a climax took her up and over a high so high she didn't care if she died when she hit bottom.

His cat raced over his skin enough that she could see him. His beauty surprised her in this moment. Lach had seen him before, of course, but this time, while they were making love, she could have sworn he told her he loved her too. As she came a second, then a third time, Lach let go of whatever tiny hold she had over herself and let herself fall into whatever well she'd fallen into as she came again.

When she awoke this time, she was alone in the huge bed. The sheets were cold, so she knew she'd been alone for some time. Sitting up, she could see her clothing lying on the floor and wondered what anyone would have said had she died, and they found the mess. Giggling, she got up and made her way to the bathroom to shower.

The hot water felt delicious over her body. She'd not realized how achy making love could make a person. Laughing again, she thought what they'd just done it wouldn't be called something so simple as making love. It had been so much more than that.

She was wrapping herself in a towel when there was a knock at the door. Telling Oakley when he told her who it was that she'd be right out, he said for her to take her time. Coming out with the towel still wrapped around her, she asked him what was wrong.

"We're going to have to work on you not thinking every time I see you there is something wrong. Nothing is wrong, love. I just wanted to come up and see you. That's all." Smiling at him, she was surprised he'd made the bed and picked up their clothing. "While you dress, I'll tell you some things. First of all, nothing bad. Your mother claimed the body of your sister yesterday and is having her buried in the cemetery with Collin. When his prints were run, they found out he had been responsible for seventeen other deaths. Your sister had been in on all but one of them. The reason I'm telling you this now is that it's going to come out in the paper in the next couple of days. Your name isn't going to be mentioned as having anything to do with any of them."

"Good. I'm glad they're out of my life and yours. What else?" He told her about how they were going to go shopping soon for things for the house. Then he mentioned the suicide note her sister had been writing and how it had been for their mother. "You're peppering good things with the bad. I'd rather you just tell me all the bad things, then tell me some good things. Then I don't want to mention them, or my mother, again if we can help it. All right?"

"I can do that. The insurance money Collin and Rita had on themselves is coming to you. Harris has made some changes to it, and I thought we could put the money in the bank for the children." She shook her head. "I had a feeling you were going to say that. What did you have in mind? I don't know the total payout of it, but Harris is working on that."

"We'll use it for people that can't have children through any kind of natural way. To help pay for some of the treatments, their insurance might not cover. I have no idea why that popped into my head, but that's as good a way to use their money as any I've ever heard of." He told her that it was brilliant. "All right. All the bad news finished?"

He said there was one more thing. "Your mother is moving away. I don't know where to, but Harris said she'd tell you if you wanted." She said she didn't. "I didn't think so, but Harris will talk to you about it when she comes over for dinner. Harris is going to keep tabs on her, so she isn't coming around here again. As far as anyone is concerned, Collin died in a horrific car accident, and your sister committed suicide. They're being buried together, but nowhere near anyone in the family."

"Okay. I don't want to know about that either." He nodded. "The babies' room is fine for now, but I'd really like them to have separate rooms. I know we have plenty of room for that. Also, I'd like to have a room for my dad when he comes around to visit. I think he will, don't you?"

"He's getting with one of my brothers to help him find a house he can live in. Something I didn't know and that he might have mentioned to you is that his second wife passed away some months ago. Frank was thinking about moving into a retirement village when Harris contacted him about you."

"I'd like that too." She was dressed then, and they headed down the stairs. "There are so many things going on in my head right now. I mean, it's been a long time since I've felt good about taking on a project. Also, before I forget, I have to be at the courthouse tomorrow for the trial with the Grays. I hope things go in my favor for this. I don't want to have one more person on my shit list right now."

Starving and glad that they had a cook to help out, she ate everything on her plate and even managed to steal two pieces of bacon from Oakley's plate. Sitting back in the chair, she felt stuffed, warm, and safe. They talked like they were a regular couple, with regular troubles and good things coming to them.

"Oh." She stood up quickly, and so did Oakley. Mrs. Marsh held her spatula like a weapon as Lach put her hands over her belly. "It moved. They moved. I felt it. Here, come feel it."

They both laid their hands on her small belly, and when Oakley smiled, she knew he too had been able to feel his children. Because they were, now and forever, his babies. Lach even knew that any other children she had, all of them by him, he would feel the same about the two she had carried for another person as he would for the children the two of them created between them.

"That's our babies there, Mrs. Marsh. Aren't we going to have the best time with them around here?" She nodded, tears in her eyes as she turned back to the stove. "I don't know about you, love, but I'm more than ready to go and get them some clothing and such for their first days in this world."

They were headed to the mall within minutes. Neither of them mentioned the things going on tomorrow at the courthouse. Nor did they ever stop holding hands, except when it was necessary. Then they held onto each other again. Lach thought having a mate and a husband was about the best thing in the world. She wondered how perfect it would be once their children came along.

Chapter 7

The courtroom was packed. While Oakley knew this was a big event for the town, he was seeing people from their little burg he'd not seen in some time. There to support their newest member, as well as hoping, he'd been told, to make a good impression so they'd be asked to babysit once in a while.

Oakley didn't know how they thought that was going to work. There was Frank, his grandda, then Fletcher, Bella's father. Five uncles and two aunts. Not to mention several friends of friends that had already put their names in the hat for their chance. They were betting on the fact that there were lots of babies coming along, he thought, what with Harris having a child and them having two. Then there was Dean and Bella's little guy, Dru.

He looked at the two people brought into the room in prison stripes, as well as chains on their ankles and wrists. Harris had found out the two of them had been nothing but trouble since they'd been arrested. Then there was the fact that Allison had been put into solitary confinement several times over the last month to keep her from hurting the other inmates. It looked like they were a pair, the two of them.

"There's that bitch that caused all this. I hope they hang your ass." No one said a word as Allie came toward the bench that she was to sit at, and close to Lach. He had to hand it to his wife; she didn't shy away from the violence of Allie. "I hope you rot in hell, bitch."

After she was seated and told to behave, Lance would turn around and glare at Lach off and on. Like that was supposed to scare her off from testifying today. The people had nearly killed Lach, and there was no way any of them were going to walk away from getting this family off the streets.

The judge, a very close friend of Harris's, came into the room amid the people moving around for a better seat. Judge Parker had spoken to Harris at great length about the things she'd found, and also how badly they needed to have these two fuck up badly here today so there would be a reckoning for their past deeds too.

There weren't any seats to be had. It was, as it turned out, standing room only in the small quiet little courtroom. They'd moved the trial to their town for two reasons. One of them to not make it hard on Lach, who was looking very banged up, thanks to Harris and a makeup team. And apparently, a change of venue had been decided on because there wasn't a soul in the Gray's town that didn't want to string the two of them up for other reasons. Apparently, they'd been making their own kind of trouble around the city, as well as the people that worked for or with them.

Once everyone was seated again, Judge Parker asked the Grays if they had an attorney. Lance stood up but was told to sit down. Henry was a no-nonsense judge, and he didn't like people messing with the rules he'd been enforcing for the last fifty years or so.

"I asked you if you had an attorney. I didn't ask you to stand up and give me a long, drawn out story as to the reasons there isn't one sitting next to you. Do you or do you not have an attorney?" Lance simply said no. "That's no sir, Mr. Gray. I'm a very important person, and it just so happens I'm the most important person you're going to meet today that may or may not keep you and your daughter out of prison. So keep that in mind when you address me."

"No, sir. I don't have an attorney." When it looked as if Lance might say more, Henry glared at him. "If you don't allow me to speak, then this is going to be a long assed trial."

"Fifty dollar fine for cursing in my courtroom. Double or nothing on how long it's going to take you to pay me for that?" Lance said nothing. "Good. It seems you can be taught. With you and your daughter not having an attorney, there will not be any coming back later to say you were poorly represented. Because you're going to be if you think you can take on this here family and not come out the loser. Are you sure, one hundred percent sure that you don't want an attorney for this trial?"

"I'm sure." There was something said under Lance's breath, but Henry chose to ignore it. "I would like to say I feel this is a waste of taxpayers' money. My daughter was poorly treated at work, and none of this would have happened had she—I mean, Ms. Russell—only done what she asked her to do."

"Are you going to do this the entire time, Mr. Gray? Or are you going to let me do my job here? I did get all gussied up this morning for this. From what I understand, there was more to this than a simple not treating your daughter well. I have a list of witnesses a mile long that are more than willing to testify about the goings on that night. Not to mention some of the things your daughter did leading up to this fateful night. Are you still sure you want no attorney to come here and help you out?"

"Yes. I'm sure." Lance finally sat down, only to have his daughter jump up as well as she could with her chains on. "My daughter is a good girl, you know. I never had any trouble with her. I don't know why she had trouble there. It's all just a misunderstanding and that woman's fault."

"I'm a great woman, Daddy. And he's right. If the dumbass back there would have just given me my dinner, then she'd not be having a hole in her head. If

you ask me, I think it's an improvement on her looks."
Henry told her that it was a fifty dollar fine for her too. "I
don't care if you put a million dollars on me in fines. She
was a total fuck up from the day my daddy hired her."

"One hundred dollar fine. We can play this all day if
you want. I know for a fact the money I bring in for people
being fined in my courtroom goes for a good cause."
Henry slammed his gavel on the desk he was behind and
glared at Allie. "Hush your mouth right now, or so help
me; the only way you're going to help your cause here is
to do so with tape over your mouth. Say another word
without my permission, and I will have you returned to
your cell. I'm not in the mood for your drama. Mr. West,
call your first witness before I blow a gasket here."

Ricky called the medic to the stand that had been first
on the scene. As he described what he'd come upon when
he'd been called to the restaurant, he talked about the
wounds Lach had received and the extent of the burns
on her back and arm.

"What else was going on when you arrived, Mr.
Tayler? Can you tell me what the staff was doing when
you arrived? Were they helping Mrs. Marshall out?" He
told him what they were doing. "What do you mean,
they were holding Ms. Gray to the floor? I wasn't aware
that she'd been hurt."

Ricky looked confused when they all knew he wasn't.
Going over his notes, he turned back to Mr. Tayler when
he said the staff was holding Ms. Gray down to prevent

her from killing, her words exactly, Mrs. Marshall.

"You mean that, even after injuring my client, she still wanted more blood? My goodness." Ricky turned and winked at them. "That doesn't sound like someone I'd want to be working with. Can you tell me what happened when you got Mrs. Marshall to the hospital?"

Mr. Tayler told them the police had arrived at the hospital and arrested her father, Mr. Lance Gray. Allie Gray was arrested, he reminded him, at the restaurant. When Ricky asked what Lance had done to be arrested, Mr. Tayler smiled.

"He threatened Mrs. Marshall as well. He told her he was going to backdate her firing, so it looked as if she'd not been working when she was hurt by his daughter. Also, and this one I figure everyone needs to know, Mr. Gray had told Mrs. Marshall to treat his daughter the same as she did everyone else. When Lach there mentioned that to him, he said he had said that, but he hadn't meant for her to get pissy with her. As you can see, that didn't go over well for her." Ricky asked him how he'd been privy to that conversation. "I was still there with the rest of my team, loading up on supplies that were ordered to be picked up. They were next to the area where our supplies are kept."

Lach stood up when she was called to the stand after Lance said he had no questions for the medic. After being sworn in, she sat down on the large chair, and Henry asked her if she was all right. Nodding, she told him she was doing better every day.

"Mrs. Marshall, in your own words, can you tell us what happened that day?" She started off by telling them that Dobie, the regular cook, hadn't been to work in a while, or she might not have been running the cook's station. "So, you were not the cook?"

"No. I was the assistant cook. I fixed up the plates when Dobie put the meal on them. Adding sauces or something else that had been ordered. I was, that night and for the previous few weeks, doing the job of two people." Ricky asked her what else she did in the restaurant. "Ordering. The food and the liquor. Also, I made up the schedule Mr. Gray was supposed to be doing and wasn't. Made sure there was coverage for all the shifts when someone called off. I'd been leaving messages for Mr. Gray for weeks about how I was working every day for the last forty, but he never called me back."

"You fucking should have kept your mouth shut about that too. She would call me three or four times a day to tell me every little thing going on. Like I had nothing else to do but listen to her bellyaching about how she was being overworked." Henry told him he had another fine added to his accounting. "Like I care right now. Because of her, the restaurant has been closed for the past month, and no one is making any money."

This went on back and forth for another twenty or so minutes. Finally, Lach told Lance to shut up and let her talk, then he could have his turn to ask questions. That, of course, didn't go over any better than Lance being told he was going to go back to jail if he didn't wait his turn. Finally, Henry had enough and ordered them both to be taken back to their cells. Lance said he'd be good from now on. He really wanted to get this over with.

Oakley was on pins and needles, hoping that the two Grays would stay. Much depended on them being able to be there so that their past crimes could be added on to what they were being charged with now. When Henry relented and let them stay, Oakley saw him wink at Harris. Thankful for friends in high places, the trial continued.

Lach finished her story by telling the room she'd had three surgeries while in the hospital. The first one was to remove the glass that had been so sharp it had pierced her skull, the second and third times were to make sure she didn't have as much scarring as they were afraid she'd have.

"Mrs. Marshall, can you tell me how many times—just an estimate—you called Mr. Gray about his daughter?" She said if she had her purse, she could answer that. Oakley took it to her and winked at her when she took it from him. "You have notes?"

"I do. I started keeping track of the things I did daily, so if anything was missing or was wrong, I could cover my own bottom. I wasn't a cook, nor did I know all that much about running a restaurant. But I didn't have anyone to call upon for advice, so I did it as best I could. Writing things down seemed to be the best way for me to keep track of the daily grind." Lach pulled out her notebook. "Allie was hired on the tenth of last month. I called Mr. Gray that night and well into the evening when she refused to do her job. I have the times here if you want those as well. In addition to the calls I made about his daughter, I also called six times to tell him Dobie hadn't shown up to work, and I was getting underpaid to do the job of two people."

This went on into the lunch hour. Henry said they'd take up where they left off when they came back at one-thirty. Things were going just the way they hoped they would, all the way up to and including making the Grays look like the worst people in the world to work for and with. There was only one more thing they wanted to be brought up by Lance, and that would seal the deal for them going to jail.

"I thought for sure he was going to be going back to jail. Then I don't know what we would have done about bringing up the past actions of Allie and her dad covering them up for her." Oakley told her he thought they'd do it soon. "I hope so. I'd really like to get some justice for the three people she killed. I guess this seeing ghosts thing is going to come in handy more than I thought."

"I hope so. They're helping Harris too." Lach nodded as she played with her food. "I believe that would do you a bit more good if you were to actually eat it instead of spreading it all around your plate."

"I'm afraid." He told her he was sorry. "No, don't be. I'm just terrified this is going to come back on me, and we're going to be paying out the ass for something I didn't do. I wish now I'd just given her the stupid steak."

"If you had, do you really think that would have been the end of it? Do you think that as she realized she could play you, she'd not be demanding more things? I don't. She and her father strike me as people that will take advantage of anyone they can. You did the right thing." She told him how the other staff were out of work. "They might be, but Harris is making sure they're getting their full pay by cooperating with her and her team on some of the other things that have happened at the place. She hasn't told me what they are, but they're going to come out soon."

After their lunch, they took a walk around the courthouse. It was getting chilly out, and there was a crispness in the air that made him want to run in the woods. The cold weather was his favorite time of the year. It was also coming up on the holiday season. Thanksgiving. It was the time of family and friends. And this year, he had a great deal more to be thankful for.

The courtroom was still packed when they arrived. Lach was called to the witness stand as soon as Henry joined them. He asked her if she was doing all right, and when she asked if she could have some water while in the *hot seat*, she called it, he had someone go to his office and get her one of his bottles. Oakley knew this wasn't a ploy — Lach had been more thirsty since she'd been at his house. Rodney said it was because it was dryer out, and she was carrying two children.

~*~

Lance was sick and tired of having the judge cut him off at every turn. It might well have been better had he had an attorney to make sure things were done correctly. But who the hell could afford one while his place was shut down? The police had done that too, shut him down until further notice. Like that was supposed to help his income.

Lance glanced at his daughter. She'd been spoilt all her life. The older she got, the more expensive things got. Not just on the things she demanded, but also getting her out of whatever trouble her temper got her into. This time, he was thankful she'd not killed anyone, but it was no less expensive. The restaurant being closed down was costing him more than he would have had to pay the family of Lach had Allie's aim been a little more on target. Maybe, like him, they would have been just thrilled to have her out of their lives.

"Daddy, when do you think we'll be able to go home?" He told her he didn't have any idea right now. "That stupid fat cow. Just look at her up there, reading off every little thing. You'd think she was a spy or something."

"I don't think she's fat, Allie, but going to have a baby." She rolled her eyes at him. "Well, I didn't want you to say something like that to her, and it come back on you. You know how people are when there is a pregnant person hurt."

He hadn't had his time to talk to Lach yet. She was still going over her notes with Mr. West. She must have spent a great deal of time, his time, writing all this shit down. Lance might bring that up if it got to the point where that was all he had left to throw at her. Time would tell, he supposed.

He wished he'd been able to afford someone like Ricky West. He seemed to be sharp and on top of shit. The only attorney he could find that would take him and his daughter on was some fuck that wanted a retainer upfront, as well as four-hundred dollars an hour. That would have included him having to drive out to the jail where they were. Then she mentioned tossing out food that hadn't been used.

"What gave you the authority to toss out perfectly good food? I surely didn't." Lach said he never gave her permission to run the restaurant either, but someone had to do it. "And you figured you were the best choice? I don't think you were running anything but into the ground."

Lance thought that was a good thing to say, but no one laughed. He thought about what she'd said about him not calling her back, and couldn't remember if he'd objected to that yet. Worth a try. He said he'd had more and better things to do with his time than to spend it all day talking to her. Lance knew he'd fucked up again when the judge banged on his desk. He wondered what it would look like if he took the gavel and beat every one of the people here in the head with it.

"While I was working two or more jobs for you, Mr. Gray, the inventory was well maintained, the staff was getting better tips, and fewer things were coming back to the kitchen that were either the wrong meal or cooked wrong. Me and the staff working there before your daughter came to work for you had your rating with the health department go from a 'C' rating to a 'B' in three weeks."

"Are you saying my daughter was dirtying things up when she worked there?" She said she was saying that. "Oh yeah? How the hell do you figure that? She was only working there for three weeks."

"In those three weeks, she only showed up for work nine days. While there, she dropped four trays of meals. Would dump her plates into the planters around the room instead of into the can in the back room, where it was sold for compost." She pulled out her fucking notebook and started reading from it. "Eighteen times—Eighteen times. I want to make sure you're hearing me correctly—she took so long to take the food out to the tables that it had to be sent back and redone. Those meals, instead of, again, taking them back to the kitchen, she must have thought that dumping them on the floor in the dishwashing area was so much better. I might add that was while the inspector was there following up on one thing we'd missed having to do with expired meat in the cooler."

"You're just trying to make my daughter look bad." No one in the room seemed to be breathing. The silence was so profound he made himself exhale loudly so he could assure himself he was still alive. "What? You think any of this is true? Everywhere my daughter went to work was the same thing. You'd think the entire world was out to get her or something."

"Your Honor, I'd like to give my witness here a little break if you'd not mind, and let me call Lance Gray to the stand. If that's all right with you."

Henry looked at him, and Lance nodded. Anything to get that fucking notebook reading stopped. Lach had been making them both look like saps. After being sworn in, he took a seat.

"I'd like to talk to you about your daughter's past jobs."

"Why?" Mr. West told him he'd opened the door to that sort of questioning when he mentioned it. "No, I didn't. I was only saying that everyone treated Allie like shit and that the Lance Gray was no different."

"That means I can question you on it. Now, where was the last place your daughter worked where she was treated so badly?" Lance didn't want to go down this road. Things might come out that he didn't want to have to deal with here. Ricky didn't smile at him now but looked at him hard. Like he was a criminal. "Answer the question, Mr. Gray. Where did your daughter work before, and what happened that you believe she was treated badly?"

"I had another business where she worked. Girls like to have spending money, and I was getting sick of just handing her my credit card each day without any kind of repayment. I love Allie. She's my only child. But she can be expensive when she wants a new outfit. I set it up so she could work in the hanger place I owned." Mr. West asked him why he'd said he *had* owned it. "Well, there was a spot of trouble there. Allie was doing a good job of making sure the bundles of hangers that came off the line were correct when the boss told her she wasn't even fit for counting hangers. Let me ask you, Mr. West, when someone says your child isn't fit to count to ten, wouldn't that upset you?"

"But he didn't say that to you, did he, Mr. Gray? He said it to your daughter, Allison Gray. What happened the day she was fired? I'm sure there was something, aren't you?" Lance nodded. Boy, had there been something. "Tell us about it, in your own words, please."

"Allie came home every night with some kind of complaint about the job. The lines were running super-fast, she told me, so she'd not be able to keep up. They timed her, only her, for her lunch hour and not anyone else. She told me how Noel, the plant manager, would have a stopwatch on him when he saw her clocking out for her meal. No one else was singled out that way. So I went to the place to see what I could find out." Mr. West told him to continue. "Noel was ragging on Allie about how she was dropping a lot of the hangers on the floor and that it was dangerous for people to get around. Also, he told her that she was too slow, and she needed to keep up. While I didn't see that her line was any faster than the others, she did seem to be struggling to keep up."

"She'd been working there for six days by then. I was told that most everyone else had picked up what they were doing in the first few hours. Miss Gray wasn't able to keep the bundles together, nor was there a good counting on them. A lot of them were short. Some were so over that it wasn't difficult to see why the manager was upset. Don't you agree?" Lance said they were picking on her from the first day. "I didn't ask you that, sir. I asked you about how upset the manager was about the shortages and overages of her bundles. Wouldn't that be cause enough to fire her? I also want to point out that you told Noel Smithson that he was to treat her like any other employee on the line. Didn't you?"

"I didn't want her to be singled out. They still did it, and that would upset her. Me too, but Allie has a temper when she's feeling like she was that day." Mr. West asked him what had happened. "Nothing that I wasn't able to fix."

"Again, I didn't ask you that, sir. I asked you what happened. In your own words, what transpired between

Mr. Smithson and your daughter?" Lance didn't want to tell anyone what had happened. He sometimes didn't believe his daughter was capable of the violence that occurred in those short few minutes. "Tell the jury what happened, sir."

"She killed him. Took a hanger off the line and beat him to death with it. Once Noel was dead, she stomped on his head until there was nothing left but a mashed mess on the floor." He looked at Ricky. "You're not human, are you?"

"I am not." Lance asked him if he'd made him answer the question. "No, I did not. You told me that all on your own. I'm sure there are other things you have on your chest. Do you want to tell us about them?"

Did he? Yes, he realized he did want to unburden himself. He figured when they got out of jail, Allie would be pissed at him. But he really needed to tell someone of the struggles he was enduring while being a good parent to his daughter.

Allie was a great girl—a great woman, he amended in his thoughts. She was just misunderstood by others. Even when he suggested they treat her like everyone else, he really didn't want them to do that. She was special to him, and he wanted everyone else to see what he saw. A strong willed, highly intelligent woman that just needed someone to treat her like he did. A goddess. Which he supposed most didn't understand either.

"Mr. Gray?" He nodded at the man and said he

did. Since he was just volunteering the information, he thought, they'd not be able to use any of it against them. This was like a sideline, he told himself. No one was going to get hurt by him telling them his deepest and darkest secrets about Allie. "Go ahead then. Tell us what you know."

Lance started out by finishing up the story about Noel. How he'd lost his business when Noel's family had demanded more than he had in cash. From there, he started at the beginning. The first time he'd had to step in and pay someone off for the way one of her classmates had tried to take back the toy in preschool that was his. Allie had beaten the little boy with a block to the point where he'd not only lost one of his eyes, but he'd also had some broken bones. Just a misunderstanding between children, he told Mr. West.

After starting at that start, he jumped around in the timeline of her life telling of this or that that he'd had to pay out for. He made sure with each story, it was understood it was the other person's fault and not that of his highly emotional daughter.

At five-thirty, Lance was emotionally drained. Who would have thought just talking about something could make him feel like he'd not had a good night's sleep in forever, and a headache? Getting down from the seat he'd been in, his legs were a little wobbly. Grabbing the table he'd been sitting at with his daughter, his legs went out from under him.

Lance laid there for several seconds. He wasn't hearing anything right then. The people in the room, all of them, seemed to have left the courtroom, and it was only him there. It was almost as if he was having an out of body experience. Or something like that. All his past deeds seemed to rush through his mind like a terrible horror movie. When he heard the screaming — his daughter's, he thought — Lance looked around to see what had disturbed her. Whatever it was, Lance didn't think he was in the position of seeing to her needs, as he was feeling sort of off for some reason. Whatever was going on, Allie was not happy about it.

Chapter 8

Since she'd been cooped up in a room all day, Lach asked Oakley if they could just walk around for a bit. He must have thought the same about being cooped up because he agreed so readily. As they walked, hand in hand, she was surprised to realize just how many people knew she was having twins, and that she and Oakley were living in one of the nicest houses on the street. Mrs. Murphy stopped them as they made their way past her shop.

"I have something I want to show the two of you. Mind, you don't have to like it, but I think you will." Oakley held the door open for her as she and Margaret, what she insisted they call her, went into the shop. "I've been working on some things here while waiting on customers. Having some new businesses around is certainly making a difference in the people that come here now. They love everything about our little town, it seems."

"I agree with you. Just yesterday, I saw Mr. Owens trimming his trees and bushes back from the sidewalk. I don't think I've ever seen him doing that himself. Usually, he hires one of his kids to do it, and they butcher them." Margaret told Oakley she'd thought the same thing. "I think I've seen a bit more late flowers being planted as well. It certainly does make it nice when you see all the fall colors."

"You bet it does." Margaret pulled out this large book. Lach had seen the kind that it was before. It was used for newspaper clippings and such. "I've been tracking our heritage, I guess you could call it. For the town, not for me. I've found some things I think might be of interest to that granddaddy of yours. Alma was in a lot of the little clubs that were the rage in the thirties and forties."

As she looked at the pictures, she saw that Margaret was right; Alma was in a lot of clubs. Her face showed up in about ninety percent of the ones that had been pasted in the book. Some of them even had Sheppard in them, along with his son, and things that he and his family had been working on.

"What's this?" Margaret turned the book toward her to look at the shot Lach was talking about. "I've never seen this place before, have I? I mean, I would think something this grand would have been kept up over the years."

The building was round and open, with a pergola on

top of it. The flowers, Lach thought, were either wisteria or morning glories. It was difficult to tell with the black and white that was there. It looked like it might have been on the square somewhere.

"Oh, it's still here. I don't think it was torn down when they were making way for the new high school. Let me see what I can find out." She went to the back room, then came back a few seconds later with the oldest woman Lach had ever seen. "This is my grandma. You'd never know she was in her late nineties. She's pretty sharp on things. You ask her what you're talking about. She'll know more than anyone else."

"I was just wondering about this place. Whether or not it was still around." Grandma, how she was introduced to her, said she was just poking around there last week. "Is it still in good shape?"

Mrs. Anderson suggested they go in the back room so that Grandma could rest while they spoke. Sitting in a well-worn chair covered in a beautiful blanket, Lach turned down a cup of tea while she unloaded the other chair and sat down as well.

"No. Not so much anymore. I think the kids around here have been putting their names all over it for so long that it's done wore down the wood." Grandma was still telling her about her poking adventure when a ghost made herself present behind her. "There was a murder done there too. Let me think on it a moment."

"It was me. I was killed there after a football game so

long ago that I'm not sure of the year anymore." Grandma provided that information unknowingly to both her and the ghost. "They never found who murdered me, but then I was considered nothing more than a girl born on the wrong side of the tracks back then."

"Lily Lynne Anderson was her name." The ghost nodded and smiled at her. Grandma continued talking about the young woman. "She was a pretty little thing. Didn't hurt anyone around here. Babysat for nearly all the folks around back then. She'd not do anything with the money on her own but turned it over to her momma when she made any. It wasn't much, but her momma could make money stretch until it screamed for mercy."

They both laughed, and Lily looked at Grandma with sadness in her eyes. Lach was more than glad to ask of Grandma what Lily didn't know, or had not been privy to about her mother and her sister.

"She had herself a little sister. No one would believe it was her momma's baby, but said it was Lily's. It wasn't. I was there when Ms. Anderson birthed both those girls. But nobody would believe me on account 'a me being so young myself. But someone, they killed her, that's for sure." Lach asked what had happened to the little sister and their mother. "Let me see. I don't want to put them out of order. The sister, her name was Rosa, died one night during the worst kind of storm. The doc back then, he'd make house calls if he had to, but he'd not make much of an effort for the poorer people around here.

Rosa got herself a cold and never got better from it. She died a little bit after her sister did, if I'm right."

"Rosa was alive when I was killed. She did have a cold. I remember that now." Lily moved around the room and stopped by the front door. "This used to be our house. I remember that too now that I've been told a little. There was a coal burner there that Momma would cook on in the winter months. Mostly she'd do her cooking outside when the weather was warmer. I remember a great many meals eaten out back on a turned over tub and rags on the ground to sit on. Momma made the worst lemonade in the world. I was glad we only had it for special occasions."

Lach looked at Grandma and then back at Lily. She didn't want to say anything for fear that it would get around that she was insane, but Lach thought of all the people she knew, Grandma would believe what she was going to tell her.

"She's here with us, Grandma. Right beside you, as a matter of fact. Lily is dressed in a green long sleeved dress that fits her nicely. Her hair is pulled back in a little ponytail with a green ribbon." Grandma asked, very quietly, if she had on her pendant from high school. "No, she doesn't. She just told me the person that killed her has it. That when he raped her, he took it before he killed her with one of the large stones around the gazebo."

Grandma just stared at the picture she'd pointed out. Not saying anything, Lach told her what her interest in the gazebo was about. She thought it would make a great place to have holiday pictures taken. As well as wedding photos, if it were in better shape.

"I took some photography classes when I was in college. I enjoyed them very much. I was thinking about going out there when the twins are born and taking their pictures around this little bit of history. I love this little town." Grandma still looked lost, or perhaps like she was trying to remember something. "Oakley and I are going to name our daughter after Alma, Grandda's wife."

"He did it, you know. My brother. I thought he had, but I was never sure enough to say anything." Lach didn't say anything as Grandma removed a small chain from around her neck and laid a pendant with the year cut into it onto the table. "I have to be honest with you when I tell you I was fearful of Lockley. To this day, I feel all shivery when I just hear his name said."

Lach looked at Lily when she spoke. "I don't know who did it. Can you tell her that for me? Even if I did, I'd never have blamed her. We were good friends in high school. I didn't know it was him." Lach told Grandma that. When she nodded, Lily put her hand on Grandma's shoulder. It wasn't as if either of them could feel the touch, but she told Grandma about it anyway. "She was forever there for me. When the other kids would make fun of me for whatever reason, I'd know she'd be right there with me fending off their meanness. I do remember Lockley, but I don't know that I ever saw him."

"He was in jail so much I'm sure after a time that's where Mom would look for him when he came up missing. He was a nasty brother, forever trying to get me into trouble for things that I'd not done." Grandma asked where Lily was, and she looked in that direction when she told her. "I'm so sorry, Lily girl. I didn't go to the police because I was terrified he'd get out of jail and kill me too. I found your pendant one day when he was caught up in something, and I needed a nickel for a bus ride to town. There it was, lying there in his sock drawer like it was some kind of favorite of his or something. I'm so deeply sorry about that."

Grandma sobbed out her sorrow as Lily did the same. The dead didn't have tears, but Lily was terribly upset all the same. Lach could see her sorrow, even feel it a little as the two of them spoke over each other. When Margaret came back to see what was going on, Grandma told her everything. But she never mentioned Lach seeing ghosts or talking to Lily.

"Uncle Lockley killed a woman?" Lach hadn't realized Margaret was a niece of the man who had killed Lily until just then. "No, you must be wrong about that. Uncle Lockley is feeble and out of his mind most of the time. But to kill someone? I don't think he'd be strong enough to do that." Lach noticed she only spoke of her uncle in terms of him doing the killing now. Not when he was younger.

"Not recently, Margaret. When we were children

144

together. He killed a woman, a child really, when he was nineteen and her just barely seventeen. Lily was my best friend in high school, and her death haunted me for the rest of my life." Margaret looked at Lach, and Grandma slapped her hands down on the table. "Don't you be blaming that girl, Margaret Anderson. Without her asking about that place out there, I wouldn't have been able to piece together why this here pendant was in his socks when he was a boy. Here, look at it. It was the year the two of us should have graduated from high school. But he killed her."

"Why would he have done such a thing?" It was Lily that answered that question. Grandma apparently had the same thoughts about it. "No. I don't believe you. I won't believe you. Why would he do that to someone that told him no? Uncle Lockley wouldn't have hurt a flea."

"He killed before too, Margaret. Mostly it was the neighborhood cats. Occasionally a dog or two. But he'd been in jail so many times back then it was difficult for any of us to be surprised by his next arrest. Even my momma, God rest her soul, shut him out of our life when he turned twenty-five. She'd not let him around me either on account of him beating me up for whatever change I had on me. I was his sister, too. Then when he was given the option of going to prison or war, Momma made him take war. I think, and I'm betting I'm right, that she was thinking he'd be killed over there and not have to return to us at all. She was that terrified of him. So was I."

Margaret sat down and didn't say anything for a long while. When she did speak, it was so quietly, as if her voice was burdened with the emotions that had been brought out today. When she looked at her, after confessing that she too had always been afraid of her uncle, she told them something else. Something that Lach had a feeling no one else in the world had ever heard before.

"I was fourteen when he picked me up from school once. He said Daddy had sent him to get me, that he wanted me to hang out with him for a few hours. I didn't think anything of it at the time, but when he pulled up in front of the old barn on the back of our property, I asked him what we were doing there. He said it was time for him to introduce me to Peter. I didn't have any idea what he was talking about until he undid his pants and pulled out his penis. He was hard, too, like he was ready to have sex with me." Grandma held Margaret's hand while she continued. "He grabbed my head and told me to kiss it. To make him feel better would make me a special person to him. I slammed my fist into his hardness and took off running to the house. I never went anywhere with him again. He wouldn't stop asking me to go places with him either, not until Mom left Dad a few years later to go and visit her momma when she got sick. I'd gotten taller while we were away. And smarter. I wouldn't even be in the same room with him if I could help it."

"I'm so sorry, darling. I should have said something

all those years ago, and you'd not have had to put up with that." Margaret said that he was scary to be around. "I'm so sorry. I'm so very sorry, child. You have no idea how much I'm sorry that he did this to you."

She and Oakley left after that. He stopped them about halfway to the car and hugged her. When he asked her if she was all right, Lach looked up at him and came to a sudden and profound decision.

"I'm going to have a fundraiser to make sure the gazebo is retooled and put back into good shape. Then I'm going to call it the Lily Lynne Anderson Memorial Park. It'll be bright with flowers and beauty. Benches so that people can go there just to relax and rest. There will be plenty of lights around it, too, so no other person can be taken there to be raped and murdered for as long as I'm alive. That prick is going to jail, I don't care how old his mother fucking ass is." Oakley laughed and said he was going with her if he was arrested. "Oh, you can bet he will be. Just as soon as I call Harris and tell her what's going on."

By the time they got to Harris's home, Lach had worked up a full steam of anger. It took her five minutes of just cursing before she could speak. When she was finished, Harris not only sent someone for the pendant, but she was going to have someone go out and arrest Mr. Anderson. It was nice to have a family like this one at her service. She had no idea what she would have done had the police, or even Harris had blown her off.

~*~

Oakley was nearly finished for the evening when Harris and Shep came over. He was always glad to see his family, and this time was no different. When they sat down with him in the living room, Harris went off to find Lach. She said she had something important to ask her.

"He confessed. Anderson did. He confessed to that crime and two others. When she brought up the part about his great-niece, he laughed and said he'd been doing his nephew a favor by introducing her to sex. Anderson said his nephew hadn't appreciated him doing that to his only child. As you can imagine, that didn't go over well at all with my wife, either." Oakley said he didn't think it would have. "The lab called right before we were sitting down to watch some television tonight, and said the pendant had blood on it—both Anderson's and the young woman's. A nearly eighty-year-old murder is finally solved. Christ, Harris was so happy she was dancing on the couch."

"Lach has been worried about it all day. She was so upset when we set out for your house that I was glad to see you both home. I have no idea what she would have done if she'd had to wait on you to come back." They both laughed. "What else, Shep? You didn't have to come all the way out here to tell me about a crime we knew to be a fact."

"Grandma Houston passed away about an hour after the police picked up the pendant. Her granddaughter thinks she'd only been staying alive to be there when her brother was finally brought to justice. I cannot believe how the crime went unsolved for so many years, only to find out that not only was there a person that knew something about it, but she'd hidden away the one thing that would convict him." Oakley pointed out that the things they had to work with now were so much better than they were even ten years ago. "Yes, that's what Harris said. She's talking to your wife about working with her. In a quiet capacity. No one would know who she is nor how she's helping."

"She was talking about that on our way home today. I think Lach was thinking she'd call up the ghosts to see what information she can get from them to help with their murders. Just to see if she could, she called up her sister. By the way, the sister isn't any nicer now that she's dead than she was alive." Shep asked if he could do it too, talk to the ghosts. "No. Whatever she got, it wasn't from me. The doctor told her there might be some changes in her memory from the head wound, but never mentioned anything like this. Lach doesn't seem to have any memory issues, which I suppose could be a bad thing or good. But then she doesn't dwell on the past all that much, she told me."

"And she shouldn't. The thing is, after she and Harris talked the day she got home, I've noticed that Harris is more relaxed about things. As if just hanging out with the other two women, including Bella, makes her more focused. I know she sleeps better too. The three of them could be sisters if you removed the fact they don't look like each other at all." Oakley told his brother he'd noticed the same thing about Lach. "I'd not point it out if I were you. I did, and Harris started asking me things like was she always so tense? Did she not sleep with me well? Just leave it alone. Trust me."

The women joined him after they both had a good laugh. Apparently, Lach was going to be working with Harris, and the money she made was going to go toward the remodeling of the gazebo. Lach had also gotten her first donation from Harris in the form of labor. It was, she told them, a good project for inmates in the jail to work on when they wanted some time outside. Harris would also pay them.

The phone ringing caught them all off guard. It was nearly eleven o'clock. Oakley answered it and sat down to make notes on whatever the person wanted. If they called this late, he was sure it wasn't going to be a social call. It wasn't, as it turned out. Ricky West said he was sorry for the late hour when he told him why he'd called.

"Allison Gray was killed today. She tried to take the gun away from one of the officers escorting her to the shrink the judge ordered. He wanted to make sure she was fit to stand trial for the murders she committed." He asked how her father was taking it. "I'm not sure I can be the one to judge him in this. He seemed to have zoned out for a bit, then I swear to you he looked happy. Almost like a huge burden had been lifted off his shoulders, and he was glad for it. I could be wrong, but I just don't understand the human mind anymore."

"I don't either. What happens with the trial now that she's no longer going to be prosecuted?" Ricky told him they would go ahead with the trial. People would still need a verdict for their loved ones. "I didn't think of that. But I can see that need. I know I would."

"Her dad, Lance, he had someone call me to come to see him in the morning. The trial has been postponed until after the funeral, of course. But Lance wants me to come in so he can make a full confession of all the crimes he's covered up for his daughter. The mother, too, I'm afraid. I'm having someone look for her now I know she's been murdered as well. He didn't know for sure when he had them call, but he thought she was dead and that Allison had killed her. We'll see." Oakley wondered if Harris would have Lach help with that one, but didn't mention it to Ricky. "There isn't any reason for you two to come back to the courtroom anymore either. I've cleared it with the judge, and he is in agreement with me. The trial is now about her deeds and his cleaning them up. Lach will be compensated for everything, first and foremost. After that, the rest of his estate will go to paying some of the other people money. That was the way Lance wanted it so that Lach will have her medical and such paid off. I think now that he's all alone in the world, he's not going to be long for this one. He's a happy but beaten man.

Don't tell Lach I said that, but I think he's going to either kill himself or will himself to death."

"That's so sad. I mean, even if he had a daughter from hell, there wasn't any reason for him to take on so. Do you think?" Ricky reminded him that he'd sort of condoned her actions by paying them off. "I suppose that's right too. I still feel sorry for him. It must have been hell having Allie doing the things she did."

"I would imagine he created most of the issues himself by shoving her off on unsuspecting people he got her to work for. After the second time it happened, I'd be looking at her, not the people that were hurt by Allie. She should never have been working at that restaurant. Not if she had a history of having a nasty temper and had murdered people. But it's done now, and all we can do is make sure people think about mental health more than they did before. Because we both know she wasn't right in the head. Someone should have done something about it long before she tried to kill our Lach."

After they spoke about the time he'd come to the house to talk to Lach about her medical bills, they ended the call. Oakley sat there for a few minutes, just looking around his home. They'd only been here for about a week, and it looked like they'd lived here their entire life. He so wished his momma was there right now. Not just to see all the grandchildren, which would put her over the moon. But to just be here with them all. Oakley had come to realize his momma was the backbone of all things family.

Going back into the living room, he smiled when he heard them talking about Thanksgiving coming up. Shep would think it was right around the corner, but in reality, it was still a couple of months away. It was only the first part of September.

When the couple left them well after one in the morning, he and Lach went up to bed. It had been a long and stressful day, and he would bet neither one of them would be up before noon. Christ, what he wouldn't give right now for just a good long sleep without any interruptions.

As soon as his head hit the pillow, he knew he was more than just exhausted. It was well beyond that. Even when Lach wrapped her nude body against his, he couldn't even manage a kiss to her. When she giggled, all he had left in him was a small smile before he just let nature take over, and he slept.

Chapter 9

Sitting at his desk the next morning, Oakley didn't remember when he'd slept so well or so late. They'd both slept until well past noon and had made love. Being energized after getting some good rest, he came three times and lost count of how many times Lach had come. He looked across from his desk when he heard a soft laugh.

"I'm sorry. I didn't realize I wasn't alone. I wonder if I even heard someone tell me you were here." The young woman looked to be in her early twenties. She was a pretty little thing. Something he knew as an adult male in this world, he would never be able to say to her. "Did you need something from me?"

"I do. I was wondering something first. You're working here all morning. Is there a reason you're not out and about the town?" He told her he was disciplined and worked from home as he would if he had a job somewhere else. "That's a good answer. I used to love the outdoors too."

He thought it an odd way of saying that, but again asked her what she needed from him. Instead of answering him, she got up and walked around the large room, stopping twice to look at a picture or the title of the books he'd brought here.

"There was a time when there was no one to help people like me. Oh, I don't mean there wasn't anyone, but it was becoming harder and harder to just get to see someone. However, the help was less than stellar and rarely did anything get finished." She looked at him. "I'm getting there, I promise you."

"You take your time with this. Sometimes I understand that getting to the point isn't always the way some people work. Why did you think I can help you?" She didn't answer him again. It didn't bother him as much as he thought it might. Being ignored when he asked a question was something he was getting used to. The roundabout way of getting to the point was his grandda's way of talking too. "I'm going to take notes if you don't mind. I take notes on a lot of things when I'm working. It's a habit I got into when a kid. I never could stop myself after that."

She sat down across from him again. "I'm dead." He asked her what she'd said. "I'm dead. I didn't think you figured that out, so I'm telling you so when I start telling you what I've come here for, you won't think me off my rocker. I can be. Silly, I mean. But not so much anymore. Since I died."

"I don't see ghosts. My wife does." She nodded at him. "No, you don't understand. I can't see ghosts at all. Lach had a head injury, and that's why she can see and talk to them. I didn't have anything hit me in the head."

"Lach could always talk to us. But when she met you, she became relaxed about herself and life, and then we came around more for her help. When she was but an infant, we kept an eye on her, knowing that someday she'd be there for us. With her family, it was difficult to approach her when she was so tied up inside. She's very relaxed now." Oakley thanked her, not even sure she was telling him he was the reason. "We—well, I—was sent to ask you if you'd be willing to help as well. Before you answer that, let me tell you why we've come to you."

"All right." He stared at her for several seconds. "Are you really dead? I don't mean to be rude or anything, but you don't look like someone that is dead. What I mean is, you're not bloody. That didn't come out right either. You're pretty, and I don't see anything like wounds on you. I have no idea why I thought all dead people had blood on them, but that's in my head right now. Blood. Lots of it."

"I died in my sleep when I was twenty. I wasn't sickly like some others I know, but I just died. It wasn't until years later, after I started talking to some of the other dead, that I learned I must have had an aneurism in my head, and it caused my death." Oakley asked her her name. "Yes, of course. I don't remember my last name. It's been so very long. But my name is Clarisse."

"I'm feeling a little overwhelmed, Clarisse. Could you, I don't know, tell me why you came to me? Just do it. I think I could handle it much better if you were to just tell me so I can process it over time." She laughed. "You have such lovely laughter. I'm betting your family misses that most of all."

"I'm sure they did. And I thank you for that. But as to why I came to speak to you, it's about Lach. She's wonderful, as you know. However, we're all a little worried about her seeing too much, and it would cause harm to her children. Bloody victim, as you mentioned. So they're not going to her unless they're not too messy." Oakley asked if they thought he could handle it. "Much better than she can, we believe. It's not just the bloody victims, but children as well. Ones abused and murdered by people that were to love them. It would be difficult for you as well—you're a kind and loving man—but you're stronger, and also not in her delicate condition."

"Okay, that makes sense. But I've never been able to see ghosts. I don't want to be rude or anything, because I'm more than willing to help, but why me?" Clarisse told him it was because he had Lach. "Yes, I do. And I love her so very much too."

"Yes, it shows in everything you do. You're a very good man, Oakley. That is another reason we've come to you." He told her he was ready to help her. "Thank you. I knew you would. As I said, you're a good man."

"I suppose there are rules. I've never asked Lach about guidelines. I thought if she were doing it wrong, someone would have told her. But we never spoke about it, or her seeing people that have gone over." He grinned. "I don't want you to think I'm not proud of her for what she's accomplished. I am. She's helped a great many people that otherwise wouldn't have been found."

"Yes, that's what she's done all her life. She just didn't know exactly what she was doing then." He didn't know what he could do to help out, but he wrote down the rules she gave him. "Also, you cannot turn away anyone if they come to you. You must try and work with them. If there isn't a resolution to their needs, then you send them away. There will be someone else out there that can help them. They have four tries to get help. If there isn't any help, they are banished from coming to anyone again."

"Are they harmed in any way if they're banished?" Clarisse told him they were just put to the back of the line until someone else was called to help them. "So it's not like a person has to give up, they just need to wait on someone that can help them. I like that."

"Sometimes, there is just no way to help some of the dead. They've waited too long to come to someone. Or it could be they've used up all their help by being a terrible person while alive. I believe you know someone like that." He asked if it was Lach's sister. "Yes, she is one.

The other is your own father. There will be no helping him because he used all his points, so to speak, while living. Some people just do not deserve a second chance at making something right."

"To be honest, I don't think about him overly much. Not even now that grandchildren are coming around for him. I think more about my mom. How I'd like to have an entire day with her, just to have her meet our mates. I know she's out there somewhere. I just miss her." Clarisse said she talked about her boys all the time. "You know her? My mom? You've spoken to her?"

"Oh, yes. Before coming to talk to you. I needed to make sure you were as nice and loving as I had hoped." He asked if he could see her. "You're not demanding that, young Oakley? You could. To have one thing that would make you help us."

"I don't think my mother would be very proud of me for demanding anything of anyone. Not only that, but I'd also not want you or anyone to get into trouble over a grown man wanting to see his momma once more." Oakley laughed. "If I could see her, I think it would be difficult for me to allow her to go away again."

"She is forever with you—with all of you. As I said, she's very proud of the lot of you. And she is forever talking about how much she loves you. Even your wives. She thinks of them as her own daughters." Oakley's heart ached then. He was so full of emotion from missing his momma that he couldn't speak. "I have hurt you in some way, haven't I?"

"No. Not at all. I was just thinking how much Shep hurt that he didn't make it home in time to see her one more time. How he has felt, all this time, that he failed her by not finding Harris sooner. Now that he's having a child of his own, I think he misses her even more." Clarisse nodded and told him that Jill did feel it from him. "Do you think it would be possible for me to call Momma so that she could see Shep once more? I don't want you to break any rules for me, but it would be nice for him, I think."

"So unselfish in your love for your family." He said he loved them, but there was nothing more to it than just giving his brother peace. "That's what you say, but in my heart and those of the others, you have given them such hope in the amount of love you have to share. Thank you for that."

After he got ahold of himself, he read over the notes once more. He was buying himself a few minutes, and he was sure Clarisse knew it. He'd never thought of helping someone like this before, and he didn't want to mess it up. He looked at the woman sitting there so quietly that he had a feeling she might be thinking he wasn't anyone for the job.

"I do want to do this." She said she'd gotten that and that he was hired. "Hired? I never would have thought of this as a job. It is, but being able to put people at peace, I think that I would like that more than anything. You've no idea how much I was beginning to think of myself as bored. Perhaps bored isn't the right word, but I was looking for something more to do that I might enjoy."

Clarisse stood up, and he did as well. "I must be on my way. It takes a great deal of energy to remain solid so that I could talk to you. There is just one more thing I would like to tell you. When you are all together, your family and extended family, the ghosts of my world travel for hundreds of miles to be close to you. The energy you give to us is so wonderful we want to feed off it." He told her they did love to be together. "And it shows. Not just to others like us, but to the world, young Oakley. Your mother, I am going to tell her straight away how wonderful a job she did in raising you six to be wonderful men."

When she left him, not fading as he thought she would but just disappearing, he sat there in his chair and thought about what he was going to be doing. Now that she was gone, however, he did have a few more questions. But nothing important. Perhaps when he spoke to Lach about his new job, he'd see if she knew the answers. Going to find her, he was going to see if she was free for a little question and answer time.

"There you are. I've been trying to remember what time my doctor's appointment is. I need to be better at writing those down." He kissed Lach on the mouth and held her to him. "Well, that was certainly a surprise. I needed it too. What have you been doing in here?"

"Working. And talking to a woman by the name of Clarisse. Do you know her?" She took a step back and stared at him. Not a pissy stare, more like a surprise. "She's a ghost. She asked me if I'd be able to help with her kind like you do."

"A pretty young woman who died in her sleep?" He said that was her. "She came to see me a few days ago. To explain some things to me about what I can do. I guess I've been doing this all my life and didn't know it. When do you start?"

"I don't know, now that you mention it. Clarisse just asked me if I'd take on some of the more messy cases, and I agreed. She knows my mom." Lach grabbed him then, pulling him so close that he nearly fell over in her enthusiasm. "I love you so much, Lach. I haven't any idea what I'd be doing if you hadn't come into my life."

"You'd be living in that apartment you rarely used other than to sleep, and bugging that poor grandda of yours to distraction." She looked at him with a sassy grin. "Or, and this is more than likely more true, the two of you would be in so much trouble you'd have to hide out once in a while to rest up. Your grandda is a pistol and a wonderful person."

"I think so too." He looked over her shoulder and saw a man standing there. Now he saw that he was a ghost and asked Lach if she could see him too. "I didn't know how this works with us both helping out. Can you see him?"

When she turned around, the man stood very still. He was a mess too, and he realized he might not have asked her with this gentleman. But Lach told him she couldn't see him because he wasn't there to see her. Pulling away from him, Lach told him she was going to hang around, just to help him if he needed it. Oakley was glad for the extra person, and they all three went into the living room so they could talk.

~*~

Longley watched the couple before him. He'd been around for a long time, even before he was murdered. But seeing these two together, the woman getting large with child, it restored his faith in humanity. Coming here, he thought, was better than just hanging around in the shadows waiting for something to happen to keep him from being too lonely and bored.

"I've been assigned to you if you can help me, Mr. Marshall." The man, a young man, told him to call him Oakley. "Thank you, sir. I'd like that. My name is Longley Cartwright. I've been gone from your world for nearly fifteen years now. Ms. Clarisse said you might be able to use me to help you get the information you might not be privy to."

"Tell me how I can help you, Longley. However, if I can help you, if you'd rather not be my helper, then we'll figure something else out. I don't want anyone to do something that they've been assigned to if that's something they don't want to do." Longley liked this man already and thought he'd do just about anything for him. Even break the rules. "You were murdered, correct? I can see that someone must have disliked you very much."

"Yes, she did — my wife. We'd been married for nearly forty years when she did this to me. I'm not saying I was the perfect man for her, but I thought us to get along pretty well. I think she thought if I was dead, she'd get all my money. I didn't leave it to her. I didn't leave it for anyone. I had me a will, mind you, but the money, it was stashed away so that neither she nor anyone else would get to it unless I wanted them to have it." Oakley asked him what he needed to be done now. "Well, I'd like for you to get it for me and spread it around. I have a list of charities I'd like to help out. And a couple of people that I know are not having such a good time in life. I'd like to be able to liven it up for them a little."

The younger man laughed, and he watched his wife leave the room. Everyone knew who Lachlan was. They'd been keeping an eye on her for some time now. She was a lot prettier than he'd been told, too — such a lovely little thing.

"Where is your money, sir?" Longley nodded. Time to get down to business. "Will I have to travel very far? Not that I mind doing that, but I'd need to make arrangements with my sister-in-law for her plane. No big deal, but I just don't want you to think I can travel like that without a flight plan."

"It's here in this town. I didn't go to anyone before

you. Nor your missus. I didn't want her to be upset with the way I was murdered." He touched his hand to the back of his head, where the bullet had shattered his skull. "The other man that was supposed to be there for the dead, he wasn't a good helper to any of us. Lazy as they come, too. But my money is right here on this property. Not too far from where we're sitting right now."

Oakley stood up, and the two of them moved to the out of doors. If only he could feel the sunshine on his face once more, Longley thought. To feel the chill in the air this time of year. It was still early enough that there would be a few hot days left, but fall, it was his favorite time of the year.

"The trees are so beautiful right now. They're getting a bit of color in them. It's like they're telling anyone that stops to see them that they're here for them. As a reminder of the summer they'd given us, here is a spot of color for you." Oakley told him that was beautiful. "Not really, but I do appreciate this time of year for the wonderous things working to make it through the winter months. My goodness, every living thing has a job to do to make sure that when spring rolls around again, they're ready. I love nature."

Longley stopped him by the little house at the back of the property. It had been updated, he saw, since the last time he'd been here. Also, he noticed that it had a new roof as well as some flowers planted around the yard.

Oakley told him that his grandda was staying in the

house now. "Not permanently. He loves to go and talk to the rest of us when it suits him. Right now, he's with my brother and his wife. They have a little boy, and Grandda is having the best time with him." Longley said he was also helping with Fletcher. "He is. I think Dru is a good distraction for them both. Is this where we need to be?"

There was a stone fence that went along the property. The big house, the one that the young couple lived in, was something he'd never been in before today. His little house, it had been nice for just himself and his wife. He'd not been aware she'd wanted something more. More, he supposed, than she wanted from him. But he wasn't going to let it get him down on how she'd killed him.

"Yes, there it is." Oakley moved the stones that the fence was made of carefully. Longley would bet, without being asked to do so, that he'd put them back too. As close to the same order as he'd taken them off. "There. Right there where that rod is planted. I did that in the event I forgot where I'd put it."

The box, a large one that he'd had especially made, was unearthed a few minutes later. He was glad to see the money he'd put in the thing was still in good shape. Not a single hole in it, nor had it rusted through. The only thing missing was the leather straps he'd had put in it so he could carry it. Not that he'd been able to do much after dragging it out here.

"Where is your wife, Longley?" The question startled him, and he laughed a little. "I'm sorry. I shouldn't pry."

"No. It's perfectly fine. I don't think I've thought much about her in a while. She's in prison now. Been there since the day after she murdered me. I guess the police thought it was a little suspicious that she purchased her a one-way ticket out of the country the evening I was found dead in my office. She didn't even get to get a refund on her ticket."

"Good. I'd hate to think she got away with taking your life." A nice boy, he'd been told, and they were right. "Here we go. Should I take it into the house or open it here?"

"Here if you'd not mind. I have me a need to see it." Oakley put in the combination to the lock on the chest then opened it up. Longley could see that it had not been disturbed. He looked at Oakley when he whistled. "I wasn't one to spend money, you see. If I didn't need it or it was something I could find cheaper elsewhere, I didn't buy it. The house, I found out the night she murdered me, wasn't to her liking. She wanted bigger, you see. It never occurred to me that we needed a large house with lots of rooms we'd not use. We had no children, you see. Not for lack of trying, I guess, but we never had any."

"I'm sorry about that. My wife and I are going to have twins in the new year. I'm so excited to see them." Everyone knew the children weren't of his blood. You'd never know it to talk to him about them. That was because the man had a good heart. A big one too, he'd bet. "Are you satisfied with what is in here, Longley? I mean, I'm just making a guess here, but I'd bet there is at the very least a million dollars in here."

"Three, as a matter of fact. As I said, I didn't like to spend money." Nodding, he watched as the younger man picked up the chest as if it didn't weigh a great deal and took it into his house, unmindful of the dirt and mud he was bringing in with it. "Your wife will be upset with you should she see this mess."

"I'll clean it up. She knows it." As if knowing they were speaking about her, she came into the room with them. Longley was a little smitten with the young woman. She introduced herself to him again as if he were a living being that she could see and told him she was going to help with the distribution of the funds. Just like that, she trusted her husband not to be fibbing to her about where he'd gotten the money. "I have a list in there that I've written down for him."

The two of them went over the list and divided up the funds as he'd wanted. The two families he wanted to help out were located, and Oakley wrote down their addresses. They were both young couples in need of a hand up. Longley knew if anyone in the world would see to it, these two would. He'd bet his last penny that Oakley would help them along more after they received the money.

Harris, a woman that scared most of the dead along with the living, joined them in the kitchen a bit later. She had a man with her, an attorney, that was going to help too. Mr. West, a man that Longley knew well, said he'd take care that the money went where it was supposed to and that neither Oakley nor him would be mentioned. Then they looked at the pile of money that was yet to be used.

"I've been thinking that over since I was murdered." He watched as Oakley repeated what he was telling them. Harris laughed and asked what else he had to do with his time other than to think. "I've been looking around this here old world. I've been keeping an eye on things. Even you and your family, young lady."

He'd meant to be funny, but she looked so sad that he told Oakley to tell her he was sorry for being flippant. She shook her head and told him she was all right. She was just emotional a great deal of late.

"'Tis the child that she carries." Oakley asked Harris if that was it. When she nodded, he did as well. "She's having a leader. Her son, he will be as great as his great grandfather and as kind and loving as his father. But he will have the strength and the knowledge of his mother that will keep him steady as the world comes to terms with his birth."

Oakley asked Harris if she knew what she was having. When she said she thought it was a boy, he confirmed it. Then Oakley told her what he'd said. Longley was a little embarrassed when she cried a little. Such a different sight of a woman who had men shaking in their boots for fear of what she'd say to them.

"Thank you so much, Longley. You've no idea how much I needed to hear that just now. I was worried he'd dislike having a hardass as a mother." Longley told her he would be the envy of all children that her son came in contact with. She was special. "Thank you again, kind sir."

"What do you want to do with the rest of the money, Longley? I think there is plenty here that if you knew a couple of more people, you could make a difference in their lives." Longley stared at Oakley. It didn't occur to him, it seemed, that he should get a part of it. He asked him about it. "I've enough money, for now, thank you. As my grandma said all the time, so long as I can light the candles and feed my family, there isn't much more in the world that I need. I feel the same way."

"Thank you for that. I would like you to take the money and use it as you see fit." Oakley asked him if he could use it to open a charity that would use the money as needed. "Yes, that's a wonderful idea. And this time, I'd like for my name to be put on it. I know that it's sort of selfish of me, but I'd like my wife to know that there was plenty of money for a nice home, but she killed me instead of asking." He thought about it for only a few seconds. "No. Don't do that. That isn't what I'm doing here. You do it like the other money, young man. My name need not be on anything. You found the money, as Mr. West said, and it should be your name on the charity."

"I'm going to name it for my mom, if you don't mind." Longley nodded, knowing that if Jill were here, she'd pop him on the back of the head for agreeing to have her name on such a thing. "The Jill Ann foundation. That's how everyone knew my momma, so that will be just fine with me."

After he left, knowing he'd be staying with the young man forever now, Longley went to find Jill. He told her of his visit with her son and how much he'd enjoyed himself. He even told her what her son was planning to do with the rest of his funds. Just like he predicted, she did pop him on the back of the head.

"You old turd. You did that on purpose, didn't you?" Longley told her he didn't know what she was talking about. "You do too. I don't think I'm going to care at all that they're thinking of me at this time. My sons, they're wonderful, aren't they? Much kinder than I deserve, but I'm ever so proud of them."

"As you should be. You did a good job of raising them, Jill. No one in the world would find fault with how they turned out. Living or dead." She nodded, thanking him for bringing her such news. "I'll be working with Oakley now. He's going to help so many of us. If you'd not mind, I'll come to see you whenever I have news from them. I'm sure it will be daily."

"I miss them—all of them. Clarisse, she told me she spoke to Oakley about Shep. I do hope he goes and talks to his brother. I so hate that he's sad. I should never have made him promise me such a thing as finding a wife and having me a grandchild. I'm ashamed of myself for saying such a thing." He told her she'd meant it in a good way. "Yes, I did. When I see him and Harris together, it warms my heart so much. She's good for him. And the others."

Longley knew he'd tell their mother everything he found out. He remembered her from when they were living. She was a kind woman that didn't deserve a man like she'd been married to. But without him, she'd not have gotten the best of the litter either. Nodding to himself, Longley thought of spending time with the Marshalls and was glad he'd been chosen to help Oakley out.

Chapter 10

Jill wasn't sure she was in the right place. She'd been told to center her thoughts on Lach, and she'd end up where she was. But there were so many people around that she was sure she'd popped into the wrong house. Then she saw her. Lach was sitting in a chair being teased by two other women.

"Hello." Jill told her she didn't want to interrupt her dinner. "You're not. I was hoping I'd get with you today." She turned to the other women. "Harris, do you have a place I can talk to this lady? I just need a little privacy."

"Sure. Use my office. If you need me, don't hesitate to call." Harris looked around the room as if looking for her. Jill had a moment of fear just then. "Don't you hurt her. I don't know what you want or need, but don't you hurt her."

"I won't." Lach told Harris what she'd said. "Is she always this intense? It must be hard to be around her a lot if she is."

Laughing, Lach got up and told her she was the nicest person she could call on. So was Bella.

Jill followed Lach through the home. Pausing only once, Jill saw the pictures of herself along the hall, with her children when they were younger. Playing in the yard. Or at a game together. Touching one of them, she felt the love and the warmth of the picture come to her. Instead of lingering in the hallway and being put to the test of her emotions, she followed Lach to the office.

"They love you." Jill nodded, unsure if she could speak just then. "They all miss you something terrible. Especially Grandda." She asked if they all called him that. "We do. In fact, when I was introduced to him, he told me that's what I was going to call him. I'm glad you came to see me. Especially today."

"Today?" Lach told her what today was. "Oh. I didn't know. Time hasn't a great deal of meaning to me anymore. Sometimes I'll find myself taking a rest and wake up to find an entire week has gone by. So, it's my birthday? I've not thought of my birthday in months."

"They're all here, all your family. Some extended as well. They decided a few days ago that they'd all be together today and that they'd share their fondest memories of you. Oakley has been writing down his memories with you. He wants to write all of them down that are said today and put them into a book. For all the children coming along." Jill was touched by their idea.

"Would you like to speak to them today?"

"Oh, no. I mean, I can't do that." She thought about saying things to her sons. "Could I? I don't want to put anyone out. And with you breeding, I don't want to take all your energy either. No. Some other time."

"I found out something just recently. That if you'd like to come and see the babies born, you can. They will be able to see you when you do. Not a single person here would object to you seeing them either." Jill hadn't had an occasion to cry lately, but now that's all she wanted to do. To sob out how much she wanted to be there to hold one of her grandchildren. To feed them a bottle. Read a story to them, or better yet, tell them about their father. To even knit them something that would be only theirs. "I'm so sorry to have upset you."

"You didn't. I only just realized how much I'm missing being with my grandchildren." Lach started to speak. "Now, I know you said I could visit them. And I will, all of them. But to hold one of them in my arms would be something that would forever make me happy. But you have given me such a gift, Lach. Such a wonderful gift that I cannot tell you in words how very much that means to me."

There was some shuffling outside the door, and she realized they were all going to the dining room. Jill wished she could sit with them. Hear about their days. When Lach stood up, she asked her where they were going.

"We're going to the dining room. If you don't want to talk to them, that's up to you. But I think you're missing a great opportunity to tell them once more how much you love them. However, you can come around anytime you wish and hear them talking about you. Listen to their pride and love for you." Jill said it wasn't fair that she died before getting to see the children of her children. "No, it wasn't. Nothing is fair when someone you love is taken from you by a senseless act."

Jill followed Lach into the dining room. When Lach sat down next to Oakley, he kissed the younger woman, then her belly. Oh, the love from these two could power a state, she thought. Looking around the table, she saw Sheppard there, holding an infant while he fed him his bottle. Jill didn't know the two men sitting next to him. However, she did recognize the illness from one of them. Dementia. She could see too that the other man and Sheppard were used to caring for him with a gentle word and kindness that she knew he had.

"I would like to propose a toast. To our mom, who couldn't be here today." Shep stood up and held his glass high. It was tea, she noticed. All the others around the table stood then and held their glasses of tea up as well. "To the greatest mother of all time. If she were here now, she'd tell me to hush up and eat before things get cold. Happy birthday, Mother. I love you more every day, and I miss you so much; I cannot explain."

They all said the same, happy birthday to her, and it

was all she could do not to run away and leave them to their meal. Her heart was so full now she knew she'd be happy for a very long time from just them wishing her a happy birthday.

Lach turned and looked at her.

"Yes. I'd like to talk to them. How do we do this?" When she put out her hand, Jill stared at it. "Will they be able to hear me simply by me touching your hand?"

"Yes." They stared at her then, everyone at the table looking in the direction of Lach. When she stood, it was as if a great pause had taken place. "Hold onto your britches, guys. I have a wonderful surprise."

When she touched her hand to Lach's, the power of her touch made her sway just a little. Looking down at the end of the table when something fell, Jill saw that Shep, her oldest son, had not just fallen back, but it looked as if he were unconscious. She let go of Lach to see to her boy.

"What's happened to him?" Lach was laughing so hard she couldn't answer. Looking around the table, just to see if anyone could answer her, she saw the stunned faces of all her boys and Sheppard too. Jill looked at Lach. "This was a terrible idea. I'm sorry, but I didn't mean for them to be upset. I've even made my oldest faint at the sight of me."

"He's a pussy." She scolded Lach for saying such a thing. "He is. He is this big leader, and there he lies, on the floor." Lach kicked Shep in the foot. "Get up, dumbass. You're scaring your mother away."

Lach finally stopped laughing and helped to wake Shep. Jill wasn't happy with her methods, but tossing a glass of tea into his face had the desired effect. Shep got up, spitting tea and cursing like—well, she didn't know who cursed like that. Taking Lach's hand again, she looked at her oldest.

"Do you want me to wash your mouth out with soap, young man?" He shook his head and said he didn't. But it was Lach's fault. "Does that make it any better? Let me answer that for you—no, it does not. Why, to think I came here today being so proud of my sons, and what do I hear? Well, too much if you were to ask me."

"Jill Ann, you've not changed one iota, have you?" She looked at Sheppard. He was finished feeding the infant and asked her to come to see. "This here is Dru. Dru Sheppard. Ain't he about the prettiest little thing you've ever done seen?"

Sheppard pulled the blankets back when she asked him to. He even took off his little socks so she could see his toes. Her need to touch him overwhelmed her, so she reached out to touch the full head of hair the little man was sporting.

"I can feel him. His warmth." Dru opened his eyes and looked right at her as if he could really see her. "Lach, can he see me? Like you said, can he really see me?"

"I was told that all children can see their family when they come around. When parents start telling them that they shouldn't is when they stop seeing. I doubt you'll ever have an issue like that when you come to see them. Not a person here will tell their children they're too old to be seeing something that they cannot." Jill watched the little boy as he stared at her. She told him she would be around if he needed her and that she already loved him. "I think your sons believe you're here, Jill."

Still clutching Lach's hand, she turned to the table. They were all staring at her, not with surprise, but with huge grins on their faces, their cheeks pink with something akin to heat. She wanted to hug them all at one time. But it was Harris that broke the spell of them staring at her.

"Shep? Tell your mother you love her, you giant lummox." Deciding to ignore the way they were mean to one another, Jill stood in front of her son. "Tell her."

"I love you, Mom. I'm so sorry." She asked him what he had to be sorry for. "For not making it home more often. For not finding my mate until you were gone. Everything in the world that made me miss you."

"Oh, son. Don't you understand? Had you met Harris sooner, your grandfather would still be sitting at Alma's grave grieving. It's all a timeline, you see?" He said he didn't understand. "In order for you to meet Harris, your grandda had to become her friend. Had he not, then Grandda might not have been called when Harris needed help. It's all in the steps that it takes to get you to where you are now. You wouldn't have come home without me dying. Then where would you be?" He told her he'd be unhappy. "You'd be lost, son. Never meeting your other half also means the others wouldn't have met theirs. You did exactly what was needed of you to make sure every one of you, going forward and now, will be as happy as I am to be here with you today."

Jill could see he was still hurt by something. Instead of talking to him more, letting his mind capture what she was saying, she turned to the others. They were all her boys. All of them right here and in her heart, like nothing had happened to take her away from them.

"Tell me what you've been up to before I fade away." It was Oakley that stood first. She didn't know what he was doing until he addressed the table.

"Power. We need to give both Mom and Lach more power." Bella asked if she had an extension cord to plug them in. "Ha. That's a good one. But I have something in mind that is a good deal safer. Love is a strong emotion. I know I'm feeling it all through my body. As I'm sure, the rest of you are. I want to try something. I want all of us to hold hands with the person next to you, and form a circle of power through our love for Momma."

As soon as Oakley took Lach's hand into his, she felt the surge of something roll over her from Lach. Each time one of them took the hand of the person next to them, connecting them to her, Jill felt like she really had been plugged into a socket.

"You're beautiful, Jill Ann." Sheppard handed Dru to his mom and stood up. "I love you all to pieces, I surely do, but this is too much for this old man. I need to have a few minutes." Then he looked at her. "You tell my Alma that I'm missing her so much. And if she has a notion of coming around to see me, I'd surely love that too. I love you very much, Jill Ann. You and yours are the best things that ever happened to me."

Sheppard left then, and she hated that she'd hurt him so. She would talk to Alma when she returned. Tell her how much her husband still grieved for her. Turning back to her family, she realized she wasn't holding onto Lach any longer, but her family could still see her.

"Tell me what you've been up to. I want to know everything." They started talking over one another, and she had to laugh. "Nothing has changed, I see. You're still the rude little boys I love."

They did tell her everything. About their jobs and how they'd been working to fix things around the town. Oakley told her about the gazebo and the murder that had been solved. Bella told her things about her life prior to falling in love with Dean.

Jill knew she'd been with her family longer than she should have been. She didn't want to leave them. Ever. But she knew she'd be around and would listen to whatever they had to tell her. She made them promise they wouldn't mourn her any longer, but to make sure they took the time to appreciate the things around them.

"Life could be gone in a flash of a second if you're not paying attention to the things you have now—family, friends, as well as a safe, good home. I want you all to look at the things around you and pick one thing daily that you're grateful for. Hold your memories close to you so that when you're here, on this side with me, you have them to keep you company. It's how I have managed to cope with being gone." They all nodded, and she nodded as well. "I need to go. I don't want to, but I need to. But don't you dare think I'm not keeping an eye on you. Understand me?"

They were telling her they loved her as she faded out. Before she was gone completely, her energy spent, she looked at Lach. Thanking her seemed to be so inept, so she did the only thing she could think of. She told her she loved her as much as if she'd come from her own body. Then she left.

Jill was exhausted when she returned to her world. Lying down on her bed, she closed her eyes. So many memories would keep her happy until the next time she could see them. Seeing her children like she had today was something she'd never forget. It had been the greatest birthday gift she had ever received.

~*~

Oakley was taking a walk when he found his grandda sitting out on his front porch. He'd been staying in the little house behind theirs off and on since he'd told him it was his. Asking if he could join him, Grandda nodded while rubbing his face with his white handkerchief.

"Are you all right, Grandda?" He nodded and said

he was just thinking. "I know. We all have a great deal to think about today. Before I forget to tell you, Harris had their new cook, Hallie, fixed you a few plates of leftovers you can put in your freezer. It was a great meal."

"It was better for the company, I'm thinking." They sat there in the dark night and listened to the forest close up for the night. "Your momma was right, you know. Her saying that the kids would be able to see her. I was remembering when I was a tyke, and my grandma would come see me at night. She would read me stories. I had to turn the pages, I remember, but I loved having her around. Then, my mom and dad, they kept telling me she was gone and that I was just looking for attention, so she faded away from seeing me."

"I'm not ever going to tell my children they're too old for things like that. I know I can say things now, and when I'm an actual father, things might be different. But I won't take their grandparents or anyone else that comes to see them away from them." Grandda told him he was a good boy. "Thanks, Grandda. You know I love you, don't you? That I just don't know what I'd do without you being around for me to talk to?"

"I'm not gonna be here forever, you know." Oakley asked him if he'd come to visit him. "I will. I didn't know I could. It has made thinking about passing on a good deal easier. Not that I'm pining away for leaving you boys, but I'm getting up there. I feel it more and more every day how old I am."

"I wasn't going to tell you this until the babies were born, but we're naming our daughter Alma Grace, after Grandma." Grandda looked at him, and he could see the tears filling in his eyes. "If you start bawling right now, we're going to be a sloppy mess out here in the dark."

"I love you, son. I surely do. You couldn't have given me a better gift than knowing you're going to honor my other half like this." The handkerchief came out again, and he blew his nose. "Let's not talk about sad things right now. I don't think my poor heart can take it."

They spoke about the upcoming fundraiser that was going to support the renovation of the gazebo. Grandda had donated to the upkeep too and said he wanted flowers planted around it that would grow up and over it.

"Wisteria? I think that is what Grandma had in your home that grew up over the deck." Grandda said it had been. "If no one else will plant and care for them, then I will. I don't remember it when it looked good. We used to go there when we were boys to eat ice cream or something we'd gotten from the dairy place."

"I don't know if I ever told you this or not, but that's where I met your grandma. She was sitting there in one of the many benches that used to be around it, looking at the flowers. I think that's why I love that flower so much. It was blooming all round her, and it made her even prettier. Whatcha doing there, boy?" He told his grandda what he was planning to do. "A memories book? Well, if that don't beat all. That'll be something. Are you adding any pictures to it? I have a whole horde of them at Shep's house. I was thinking on bringing them here so I could take a gander at them once in a while."

"That's a wonderful idea, Grandda. I'd love to put pictures in it that the rest of us might not have." Oakley thought his grandda was the greatest. He proved it time and time again. "I was also thinking about putting in some town pictures. I don't suppose you have any of those from when you were younger."

"I do, as a matter of fact. Your grandma, she sure knew what to keep. It ain't a bit like today, where a person takes a picture of everything they eat and passes it around to other folks. You just had to think about what you might be taking a picture of, so you'd not waste your pictures on silly things when you really needed to take a picture." Grandda laughed. "I'm betting right now Dean is in his bed looking over the pictures he took of me and Dru tonight. And that Bella is missing that boy so much she's gonna go in there and pick him up and bring him back to bed with them. Darndest thing, having a little baby around. Sure can make a person think about life."

"I know I do. I'm also a little afraid for my kids to be born. Not of them, but what the world might be like when they're ready to go out into it. I know they're not born yet, but it still makes you think." Grandda agreed with him. "Then there is all the things going on with us helping the dead. I love helping, but I'm so afraid I'm going to make the wrong decision about them."

"You're not going to. If they thought you might, they'd never have come to you in the first place. Whatever you're doing for them is a darn sight better than anyone had been doing. Lach, she told me about the other person that was helping them. Sorriest bunch of idiots I've ever heard of." Grandda had always been able to tell it like it was. Oakley loved him for that. "You get yourself on back to your own warm bed. I'm going to be heading up to mine now too. Talking to you, it's been nice. Took my mind off being an old worthless man tonight."

"Grandda, I hope you really don't feel that way. You're about as worthless as my love for Lach is. I need you, and I'm positive the rest of us do as well. You're our connection to those that have gone on. The backbone of this family." He grinned at his grandda. "I don't have to tell you how much you're going to be in our children's lives, do I? They're going to be so happy to see you every day that it'll be difficult for us to spend any time with them. But I already know what I'm going to do. I'm going to barge into whatever you have going on with them, so I too will have good solid memories of you and them together."

"You're all right, Oakley. I needed that tonight. Seeing your momma, it brought on memories and aches of losing her both at the same time." He stood up and hugged his grandda, and knew that from now on, he was going to be with him every chance he could. The man was a wonder. "I love you too. Now, do what I said. Get yourself home, and I'll be seeing you in the morning. We've got that appointment to go to with your missus. I'm going to see my next grandbabies, and I'm about as excited as a cat is in a room full of old people just wanting to hold her."

As soon as he got back to the house, he wrote down his grandda's comment. There were plenty more of those that he'd been thinking about. They were going to be an entire chapter in his book. Grandda Quotes. That was going to be the header for it.

"Everything all right." He pulled Lach to him and hugged her tightly. "I guess it is. I saw you out there talking to Grandda. Is he doing all right too?"

"He is. Feeling his age, I think. He actually told me he was feeling worthless tonight. I fixed it for him. I think seeing Mom was just a little too emotional for him. Got him to thinking about his own age." Lach asked him if she should go out and knock him around a little. "I think he's all right now. He suggested I put pictures in my book. I've never written one before, but this is going to be epic. Even if it is just for the family."

"Why?" He asked Lach what she meant. "You were saying you wanted to incorporate the town and its growth in the book. Grandda has pictures too, I'm betting. Why does it just have to be for the family? I might well enjoy just looking at the memories of someone that has been here his whole life, even if I wasn't family. You shouldn't settle on just for us, Oakley. I can see this thing as a keepsake for other people you might mention in the book. Storefronts that might have a family name on them."

"Will you help me?" She only had to smile at him, and he had his answer. "I'm betting with this thing we can do that we can call up others, just for their memories about a certain picture Grandda has. I like that idea."

"I do, as well. It'll be something people who have been here as a visitor will enjoy too. I think you should put pictures of the gazebo as it progresses to looking good again. The Christmas lights along the street now and back then. Yes, I can see this book having sequels too." He told her he'd not written the first one yet, to wait a little while. "Oakley, you're going to have so many people coming to you about their stories and their families that you're going to be busier than a one legged man in a potato sack race. I heard Grandda say that the other day."

He wrote it down. "Grandda and I are going to go over the plans for the gazebo in the morning. I guess someone in the courthouse found the original plans for it, as well as pictures of it while it was being built." She asked him as they headed up to bed if there might be people in the pictures. "I never thought of asking. But when you say that, it makes me think you're right about others maybe wanting to see the book. If my relatives were mentioned in it, I'd want to get a copy of it too. How did I not know you were brilliant?"

"I hide it well, I guess." She got into bed, and he could see how exhausted she was. "Today wore me out. I don't know what I was thinking when I brought your wonderful mother here."

"Because, my dear wife, you're more brilliant than I first thought." He kissed her, then her growing belly. "Good night, my babies. Remember that Daddy loves you already more than I thought possible."

Lach fell asleep quickly. Oakley couldn't get enough of just watching her. At four months, she was beginning to show more and had started wearing his shirts around the house, and he loved it. Lying back on his side of the bed, he thought about the book.

He knew he'd do it. Just getting started was something that he was having difficulty with. Did he put the pictures he was planning to use all in one place or everywhere in the book? A title was also giving him fits. Each time he thought he had a good name for his book, he'd think of something else. The one that he'd thought of while sitting with his grandda had been one he thought was the best. But he had not run it by Lach to see if she liked it too. *Marshall's Shadow* might be the one he picked.

As he settled down in the bed after putting his notebook away, he rolled over and pulled Lach closer to him. Tomorrow he had a busy morning, and then in the afternoon, he was going to talk to the woman Harris had suggested in getting ideas for his book. Like a kid at Christmas, he couldn't wait to see what she thought of his idea. If she thought it was stupid, then he'd just go back to his original plan and make it for his family. They'd enjoy it if no one else ever saw it.

Falling to sleep, he knew that once he woke, he'd be a day closer to holding his children. A day closer to getting projects finished. And more than anything, he'd get to fall in love with his wife again and again.

Chapter 11

Rodney tossed the ball he was using as a stress reliever against the wall. Not that he was stressed, not really, but he was bored out of his mind. He looked at his calendar again to make sure there wasn't anything that popped up while he'd been sitting there.

"You keep that up, and I'm going to come in there and beat you with that ball." He grinned when Adaline yelled at him from the front office. "I told you that you're going to have to get yourself a hobby before we even got this place open. People have to find you before they'll come to let you see their bits and pieces. How you doing on finding the books I told you about?"

"They're going to be here tomorrow." She said that was good. "I know you said I could have them right away if I loaded them on a reader, but I need to touch the words I'm reading in a book. I love the smell of them too."

"You're weird. Anyone ever tell you that before?" She came into the office with him, and he smiled at her. "I have a big favor to ask of you. Now, I want you to think on it before you just say yes. I know you will because you feel you owe me something. You don't, so let's just leave it at that, all right?"

"All right. You seem serious all of a sudden. What's happened?" He loved Adaline. She was his rock since he'd done his residence at the local hospital. "Are you ill? You don't smell like it."

"What a way to tell someone that. Like I smell or something. It's a small wonder some nice woman hasn't taken you to task the way you talk to the fairer sex. No, I'm not ill, and I don't stink either." He said he didn't mean that. "Yes, you did. You always mean what you say. Now listen to me good before I hit you upside the head like your momma used to do. The school is having some trouble there. Not with the teachers, but with the health staff they have. I've heard from Mrs. Briggs, the principle, that the woman won't treat the kids that are poor. Nurses are supposed to be above how much their patients make. But this one, Nurse Lannie Jackson, is a pain in the ass. Those poor kids get just as sick as the rich ones do, don't they?"

"They do. Sometimes more than the rich kids because they don't usually get a good meal before they go out to wait on the bus. Tell me what it is you need me to take care of." She left him there and returned a few seconds later with a box. "Please tell me you didn't steal all the school records, Adaline."

"I didn't. Mrs. Briggs handed them over to me when I said I'd have you look at them." He pulled the first file out of the box and looked at the record. "That's Mrs. Handle's boy, Ronny. You know him. He's the one that lost his daddy a few months back when the wall he was working on collapsed."

"It says he's faking being ill so he can be in the nurse's office when they're having tests. From what I'm reading here, they must have more tests at school than when I was going there. Like every day." Adaline told him he was just a drop in the bucket for being ignored. He took another file out, laying Ronny's to the side. "Alice Sharp has bruises all over her arms and back. She actually wrote in her file that 'Alice is a fat, clumsy fuck.' Who makes those sorts of comments about a child? Not to mention, writing it in their permanent file?"

"That sounds like something she'd do. The other day I was over at the school when my grandson called me because he'd lost his lunch money. I heard her talking to one of the kids in her office. She didn't even close the door while she spoke to him. Lannie told that little boy he needed a bath, that he should be going to the river to clean up. Maybe he'd slip and fall in while he was at it. I was so shocked I went right in there and grabbed him right up. Why would she tell him to fall into the river when it's so cold outside? I have to tell you, Rodney, she's going to hurt one of them kids sooner or later."

He stood up and pulled on his jacket. Adaline asked him where he was going. "To the school. This shit is going to stop right now. Even if I have to fire her and work there myself." She told him she thought that was a better idea. "You didn't come in here to ask me to work there?"

"No. I wanted you to go and treat the kids she's not. But this is so much better. I'll come with you. *We* might have to have a coming to Jesus meeting with her, and I want to be your back up."

Rodney laughed all the way to the school. It wasn't that far from his office, so the two of them walked over. He noticed that Adaline had his bag.

As soon as he was buzzed into the school office, Mrs. Briggs came around the corner and thanked him for coming. He didn't know what she meant right away, but apparently, they'd been expecting him. When he asked where the nurse was, he was told she'd not shown up today.

"I was under the impression she was supposed to be here every day." Mrs. Briggs told him she was supposed to. But she only came in once a week now. "What if someone is hurt or sick? How does she expect to treat them from wherever she is?"

"She said there isn't enough going on here for her to have to sit around all day and be bored. Also, I was told she was to help out in the office if there wasn't much going on. Lannie told me that if she wanted a desk job, she'd have taken one. That girl is going to be in trouble next year if her contract is renewed as a nurse to this area. I'm hoping that Lannie isn't renewed, but I don't get a say in matters such as that." Rodney asked her to call the woman and tell her that he said to get her ass in there. "I can do that. But she's not going to like it."

"She's going to like it even less when I fire her." Mrs. Briggs asked if he could do that. "I can. I was asked to oversee the school nursing programs here in the event there was a breakout. I was also told if there were problems with any of the nurses here, I was their report to, and I had full authority to fire them."

"Well, why didn't we call you sooner?" Mrs. Briggs asked one of the staff if they could make the call. "If she gives you any crap, I'll speak to her."

"If she gives you any crap, I'll speak to her. Might save her a trip here if I fire her over the phone, don't you think?" While they were looking up the phone number, he was calling the one person on the board he knew might back him up. After telling Harris what he was doing, he asked her to come there. "I'm at the elementary school now. Can you meet me here?"

"I can. But I'm bringing Bella with me. She and I are both on the board. I was going to ask Lach to join us. We need to whip this place into shape before our own children go there." He agreed with her. "I'm picking up Bella and Lach now. We'll stick around if you need help in the office."

Good. He would have a nurse should he need one, and help in the form of talking to the kids. While he was waiting for someone to hand him the phone for Lannie, Mrs. Briggs brought out several large, heavy boxes on a cart. He asked her what this was.

"This past summer, all these things were donated by your family to hand out to the kids. Not a single one of them got the hair and toothbrushes, nor did she hand out any of the things that had been donated. I have baggies filled for each and every student here ready to be given out on the first day of school. There is also a printed up list of things a child might still need that was put along with the other things in there. Like pencils and such, the family might not be able to afford."

He called Shep. "I need you to go by the department store in town and pick up some items for the school." Shep said he'd be happy to. "Take Grandda with you. He might well enjoy this."

Rodney read off every item on the list and told him to buy out whatever they had in the form of a donation to the school. Shep laughed and asked him if he was going to be in charge of all this stuff. He didn't know, but it had been lying around too long, waiting for someone to figure it out.

He was handed the phone just as his sisters-in-law showed up. Lach took the phone from him and asked who it was she was speaking to. After figuring out who it was, Lach apologized in advance to the staff in the office.

"What the fuck do you think you're doing at home right now? There are children at this school who you were paid to care for waiting for you." He didn't know what Lannie said to Lach, but he would bet she'd be careful in the future of saying it to someone else. "You *think* no one needs you today? You *think* you're doing a good job here? Honey, you are so fucking stupid I might have to have you put into the world book of stupid people soon. We, as the city, do not pay you for taking time off. As of right now, you're fired. If you have a problem with that, then please, by all means, come down here and voice your concerns. I'll be here with Harris and Bella, just waiting for you to show your face here again."

She handed the phone to Mrs. Briggs. "She's upset. I don't care if you think this is the wrong way to go about this, but if you agree with me, then hang up. She'll show up, and I'll have her arrested. She's been fired, and that's the end of it."

"Remind me never to get on your bad side." Lach grinned at Mrs. Briggs. "Are you really going to be on the board, Mrs. Marshall?"

"It's Lach, and I am. I want you to call any of the three of us directly if you need anything. I mean anything. Air conditioners fixed. A fridge breaks down. Hell, if you need bottled water for the Friday night football games, you'll get it. As I was telling these women here, this is our school for our kids, and we need it to be in good shape for them." Mrs. Briggs told her that as of the last month, they needed all three of those things. "All right. You write it all down, and between the three of us, we'll get you fixed up. But, as I'm sure the others will agree, no one knows who donated things. It'll be better if they think it's coming from the town as a whole. You might want to thank some anonymous people in the next email that goes out. Say something like the people will double their donations if fifty people donate their time to some of the things going on around here."

"Oh, I like you."

Harris hugged Lach and told her she'd done good. Mrs. Briggs left to go to her office to work on the list. Sandra, one of the aides in the school, asked what they wanted to do.

"Bring in the first grade, and we'll work from there. Shep said he'd bring the stuff he's picking up to the back door to be loaded in here." Rodney looked at his sisters. "You guys are the best. I hope you know that."

Within half an hour, he had twenty-five kids lined up against the wall and was giving them quick exams. Lach followed behind him, giving each kid a packet that contained toothbrushes, paste, and other personal items for the entire family. She also spoke to each child to find out what sort of things were going on in their home. Bella was making notes about that on each file. Things were moving now.

By the time he was on the last grade at the school,

Shep and Grandda had off loaded the things that were on the truck. They ended up making several trips to the store, and Shep had put in an order at a larger store for things that weren't on the list. He had ordered backpacks to be given to the kids, and someone was coming in to help measure the kids for coats and boots if they needed them. Rodney didn't think there was a child in this school that didn't need winter boots.

"How're the other schools doing?" He'd not thought of the middle or high school and what sort of things they might need. Rodney was thrilled to have someone thinking about them too. "Do you know if they might need a nurse as well?"

"The high school has a good one. She's my granddaughter, and she knows better than to let them down." Rodney laughed with Mrs. Briggs when she answered Adaline. "The middle school, I don't know. I know they had a nurse working, but I couldn't tell you anything about her. You might have to check on that too."

Harris left to check on the other two schools as he and the others finished up the exams of all the children. She'd also made notes on the kids that were going to need more than just a quick exam like he was doing.

"The school was supposed to have an eye doctor come in. Do you know if one was scheduled?" None of them had heard anything about that. "I'll take care of that when I get back to my office."

One of the secretaries was making notes for him too. Adaline was still working with the cafeteria workers to find out if the kids were getting the breakfast program. He thought there was some sort of grant that could help defray the costs of feeding the kids the first meal of the day.

At half-past six, exhausted yet delighted with the progress they'd made, Rodney sat down with Mrs. Briggs to go over the list of things the school was in desperate need of. She told him the kitchen area needed to be upgraded completely, and that most of their tables and chairs weren't in good condition.

"Don't feel you have to do all of this for us, Rodney. It's a great deal to take on. Paying for it all on your own will put you in the poor house." He said he'd talk to his family about a fundraiser for most of it. "Good luck with that. Most of the people in this town have been out of work for some time now. They could use a boost up as much as this school does. We've tried before to get the parents involved, but they just don't have the funds to help out."

He thought about what she told him all the way back to his office to get his car. The town would do so much better if there was extra income for the people. It was that same trickle-down theory that he'd been seeing a great deal lately. Without working folks in town, the restaurants didn't do well and would close up. And so on down the line. He needed to have something big come to town to make jobs for everyone. Rodney thought he needed to speak to Harris. She had a head for such things.

~*~

Rebel looked over the paperwork she'd been handed when she came to the school meeting. Her niece and nephew went to school here, and since their mom wasn't able to take time off her job, Rebel said she'd go. There were a great many people there, more than she thought were parents of the children.

After the meeting was called to order, she listened to a woman talking about what they'd found out about the nursing staff that worked for the schools. Harris, she thought her name was, said they'd been doing a piss poor job of taking care of the elementary children. What they'd done about it and how the donations were pouring in to make things better here. Rebel had gone to school in another country but knew there were big struggles to keep good teachers on the payroll.

Each person that was to speak to the crowd of several hundred people had positive things to say about the teachers but also pointed out that they needed more than just a chalkboard and paper. They needed volunteers too. People that could spare an hour would help a teacher get papers graded and things in their rooms put back in order at the end of the day.

"Aunt Rebel, can you come into my class and help out? Mrs. Montgomery is doing her best, but she gets cranky if she gets too much going." Rebel asked Todd what the teacher had said that made him think she was cranky. "Nothing. She just looks tired. I think she's really old too. Older than you even."

"Thanks, kid." He laughed when she did. Then Angie spoke up. She was in the first grade and was in love with her teacher. "What do you think they need in the school, honey? More breaks or something?"

"Computers. They only have one in my classroom that works. I like using it, but it takes forever for my turn to come around." She nodded, thinking of the computers they had in their home. "I can do all my homework on mine at home, but the teacher's doesn't work all the time, and I get a late point when she can't pull it up."

Rebel made a mental note to get them a printer so that Angie could turn in her homework on time. The kids around them were telling her what they needed, as well. Finally, when Rebel realized how much they saw as opposed to the teachers, she stood up to be heard.

The man standing up there asked her what she had an idea for. "Not so much an idea, but a concern. I have a niece and nephew that go here. I'm hearing from them that computers don't work most of the time. That the Internet is so slow, they can't turn in homework on time that they've done at home." He asked her if she'd like to meet with him after the meeting. "Sorry, but I work the night shift at my job. I can't be late any more than homework can be."

The man, Rodney he said his name was, said he'd

meet her at any time she could get away if she'd work with him through the kids. She didn't want to take up that much time working on this, but Angie begged her to help out. So she found herself giving out her personal phone number and receiving Rodney's before she left. Somehow she felt like she'd been sucker-punched when he handed his over.

On the way back to their home, the kids were telling her about how Doc Rodney had given them toothbrushes and stuff the other day. And that there was a *big old room* with supplies in it just for the kids to have.

She knew who the Marshalls were. Anyone that was in town for less than a minute heard how the Marshall family was the big deal around. Rebel thought she would give the list she had as well as the notes she'd taken from the meeting to her sister-in-law. That way, she'd not have to be around the other man too much more. He was good looking, but she was just getting out of a sour relationship and didn't need anything more fucking up her life.

After tucking the kids into bed, she made her way to Sheila's kitchen. It might well have empty cabinets all the time, but she did a good job raising the kids like she was.

Her brother, Thomas, had died a few years ago, just after Angie had been born. The insurance company didn't pay out, and Shela and the kids depended on her to help them out each month for food and bills. She didn't mind. Rebel loved the kids, and Sheila as well.

Tomorrow when she got off work, she was going to go down there again and see what the fucking hold up was. At eleven-thirty, the nighttime babysitter showed up, and Rebel was free to go to work. She hated working nights, but at the hospital she was working at, those that weren't born in this country didn't get to pick what they wanted. She hated the staff there more than she did the situation Sheila and her children were in.

Going into work, she was met with hostility and anger. Not from the people in the emergency department that needed help, but the people she had to work with. Rebel was tired of the same shit daily. They would hide files from her. Set up patients that were ready to go home to have stitches put in. Some of the nurses would steal her things right from her locker. Tell some of the patients that she was a nurse, not a doctor, as she had told them. The fun they'd have with her accent. Stupid shit that just got in the way of her working. At the end of her shift, she was turning in her resignation. Enough was enough.

AWARD WINNING, BESTSELLING AUTHOR

Kathi Barton, a winner of the Pinnacle Book Achievement award as well as a best-selling author on Amazon and All Romance books, lives in Nashport, Ohio, with her husband, Paul. When not creating new worlds and romance, Kathi and her husband enjoy camping and going to auctions. She can also be seen at county fairs with her husband, who is an artist and potter.

Her muse, a cross between Jimmy Stewart and Hugh Jackman, brings her stories to life for her readers in a way that has them coming back time and again for more. Her favorite genre is paranormal romance, with a great deal of spice. You can visit Kathi on line and drop her an email if you'd like. She loves hearing from her fans. aaronskiss@gmail.com.

Follow Kathi on her blog: http://kathisbartonauthor. blogspot.com/

www.ingramcontent.com/pod-product-compliance
Lightning Source LLC
Chambersburg PA
CBHW061221170626
46809CB00007B/2547